D0892239

# FLYING THE BANNER

*Short stories from Clare's teenage writers*

# FLYING THE BANNER

*Short stories from
Clare's teenage writers*

Compiled and edited by
Ré Ó Laighléis

MÓINÍN

in collaboration with
Clare County Library and Clare Arts Office
and with the generous financial assistance of
Judith A. (Foley) Badman

First published in 2012 by MÓINÍN
in collaboration with Clare County Library and Clare Arts Office

MÓINÍN, Loch Reasca, Ballyvaughan, Co. Clare
Tel/Fax: (065) 707 7256
E-mail: moinin@eircom.net
Web: www.moinin.ie

Copyright © The individual authors, 2012

The individual authors assert the moral right to be identified as the authors
of the respective stories in this work.

All rights reserved. No part of this publication may be
reproduced, stored in a retrieval system, or transmitted,
in any form or by any means, be that mechanically, electronically
or any other without the prior permission in writing of the publisher
and the individual author(s).

This book is sold subject to the conditions that it shall not, by way of
trade or otherwise, be lent, re-sold, hired out or otherwise circulated
without the publisher's prior consent in any form of binding or cover
other than that in which it is published and without a similar condition
including this condition being imposed on the subsequent purchaser.

A copy of this book is available in the National Library of Ireland,
in the libraries of Trinity College, Dublin, and in the libraries of the
non-constituent and the constituent colleges of the National University of Ireland.

A CIP catalogue record for this book is available from the British Library.

ISBN 978-0-9564926-9-2

Set in Palatino 10.5/14

Cover creation and design by Link Associates
Edited by Ré Ó Laighléis
Layout and typesetting by Carole Devaney
Printed and bound in Ireland by Clódóirí Chois Fharraige Teo., Connemara,
Co. Galway, Ireland

# Contents

# Dedicated to the Memory of Dermot Foley
# (1907-1991)

Dermot Foley was born in Dublin in 1907. As first Clare County Librarian, he was a great protagonist of the short story. Two of his closest friends were the great Irish short story writers, Frank O'Connor and Seán O'Faoláin. Hence, support for the publication of this book seems a fitting way to honour him for all he did for the Clare Library Service.

Dermot Foley's career started in Dublin at Rathmines Library. He progressed to the Pembroke Library in Ballsbridge, where he was assistant to the librarian Michael O'Donovan – better known as Frank O'Connor. In 1931, he was appointed to Clare, where a small room in the Courthouse served as his first library. From then until 1954, when he left for Cork City Library, he developed the Clare Library Service with great enthusiasm, and that despite many setbacks. He did all he could to encourage a love of literature and learning, persuading Clare County Council to provide a library van, to carry books all over Clare, driving it himself and – for want of an assistant – closing the library in Ennis while he did so. Slowly, he built up a library presence in most of the small towns, eventually managing to rent empty shops and have them fitted out as libraries in every town in Clare.

The enthusiasm of this inner city man was tremendous. On one occasion, Dermot drove the green library van to Ballyvaughan to engage a gathering of farmers, to whom he made a presentation on the benefits of books. He had made and set up a display of posters and instructions on advanced farming techniques, impressing on his audience that information on such was to be sourced through the reading of library books. He also founded a drama group in a hall near the present-day County Library HQ and was so successful that he was invited to start more groups in other towns, which he duly did. Thus, he spread his love of plays, enthusing many young people, widening their horizons and nurturing in them the self-confidence to achieve more in their lives. In the talk *A Minstrel Boy with a Satchel of Books*, delivered at the University of Michigan, Ann Arbor, in 1973 and subsequently published in the *Irish University Review* (Volume 4, 1974), he drew from his Clare experience.

In 1951, Dermot Foley and a colleague were appointed by the Government of Ireland to survey the state of libraries throughout the Irish Republic. This was a groundbreaking body of work. As a result of this, in 1960 Dermot was appointed the first Director of An Chomhairle Leabharlanna, the Irish Library Council, with the task of developing the library service throughout the 26 counties. During this time, he negotiated the purchase of the Presbyterian Church and Manse in Ennis, thereby adding to the present-day De Valera branch and also providing for the community an independent Local Studies Centre. The library service in Clare thus progressed immeasurably from the little room in the Courthouse to the vibrant, extensive service that it is today.

**Judith A. (Foley) Badman**
*October 2012*

# Foreword

Clare County Library and Clare Arts Office enjoy a strong tradition of promoting artistic endeavour in every format. This is particularly reflected in a long and dedicated commitment to promoting literary skills and the joys of reading. Pushing the boundaries of traditional library service delivery into publishing books, guidelines to literary promotions, a transatlantic reading challenge and the continued support of activities centred around both children and teenagers, the library service endeavours to involve its community of users and to celebrate its achievements in a fitting manner. One such achievement is the publication of this book.

Over a period of three years, Clare County Library and Clare Arts Office have engaged in a collaborative venture in creative writing with well-known and highly acclaimed local author, Ré Ó Laighléis. In the course of those years, seven second-level schools in the county nominated students to participate in this skills-based project, conducted under the guidance and discipline of their accomplished tutor. With an innate feel for the subject, and drawing from a wealth of writing and mentoring experience, Ré instilled in each participant the ability to hone and shape each story in the collection you now see before you. We are indebted to Ré, not only for his dedication to this project, but also for making the experience one that has been fun-filled and highly productive.

A debt of gratitude is owed also to the library staff in Shannon, Kilrush and Ennistymon Libraries, who facilitated the creative writing workshops, and to our funding sponsors, MÓINÍN, O'Mahony's booksellers, Judith Badman and Clare Arts Office, without whom this publication would not have happened. A special 'thank you' to our Children's & Teenage Librarian, Ms. Patricia Fitzgerald, whose background work sometimes goes unnoticed.

I hope you enjoy reading these stories and I wish all our aspiring authors success in the future on whatever path life takes them.

**Helen Walsh**
*Clare County Librarian*

# Introduction

Four years have passed since the conception of this project. From its first mooting, it was a concept that compelled enactment. In no time at all, the notion gained legs and took on an impetus that would show its realisation to be nothing if not undeniable. What was initially a one-year project morphed into two, then into three, its increasing intensity and growth being a function of the small number of key and visionary principals who stood unflinchingly at the helm of a ship that would take its passengers and crew on an adventurous and searching voyage into the world of creative writing. But more on such people anon.

My regard for the young writers whose stories appear in this collection is immeasurable. I have had the immense privilege of having them committed to my care for what, in each of the three six-session years of this coursework, proved to be a period of great intensity and remarkable industry. To the last, each and every one of them has impressed me hugely with their honesty, their openness, their ability and eagerness to learn, their hard work, their pride in place, in school and, most particularly, in family. They are a reflection of their friends, their teachers, their siblings and, not just their parents but, indeed, their grandparents also. They are the bearers of the banner that we variously term tradition, heritage, Irishness. *Gael mise – nach uasal san!* They have done you proud, one and all. And, in so doing, they are aware that what talent they may have is every bit as much of their parents and grandparents as it is of themselves. They have taken nobly of what there was to learn and, through their accomplished stories, they now pass on the richness of their endeavour to their contemporaries and to generations yet to come. What they have done is no small thing. What they have done matters very much. What they have done will abide and will swell the vats of tradition, heritage and Irishness from which they themselves have supped. I am inordinately proud to know these young people and to have had time with them.

It is important for the reader to realise that, at their time of writing, these young enthusiasts ranged in age from a mere 12 to 17 years and that the task they took on is arguably the most daunting of all in the realm of literary endeavour. Amongst professional writers, the Short Story is widely regarded as being the most exacting of literary talent and craftsmanship. Of its nature, it requires a minimalism, a succinctness, a precision of skill and application that cannot allow for superfluousness of any sort. Its elements of structure, characterisation, plot, narrative and dialogue can only work to optimal effect when they have been honed and whittled and crafted to a fine and unsparing end.

It may be enlightening to reveal a little of what has brought these writers to the point where their stories are not only deserving of publication but, indeed, actually command such. On each of six successive Fridays, the writers attended a two and a half hour instructional session at which, respectively, instruction was given in one particular skill element of short story writing. This instruction was complemented by the use of and exposure to tried and tested material in which optimal use of that skill element was evident. The writers, from the outset, were further presented with the expectation that, in advance of the third session, at the latest, each would submit to the course director a story of his or her own choice, to which the skill elements learned to date would be applied. It is important here to point out that at no stage in the course of learning was a writing topic given to the writers by the director. The selection of topics was solely and entirely the decision of each individual writer. The belief here was that what they would best write would be that about which they knew and/or that in which they were interested. Having submitted their stories on a weekly basis, the course director would then take them away for reading, written comment and 'suggested' amendment(s), but never himself actually making any qualitative changes in the scripts – the ifs and hows and whats of that being exclusively the will of the young authors – and return the marked manuscripts to the writers.

And so, each year, the process would go on over the course of six sessions, with the imparting of a new skill element each week and the continued honing by the writers, as they assimilated and applied those skills to the developing piece of work, ultimately culminating in the finished story. Throughout each session, in the group context, attention would be given to the more salient issues arising in the various stories as pertained to the application of the most recently imparted skill and the cumulatively applied skills. Also, within the sessions, the writers would both read their stories aloud and/or interchange them for silent reading by their peers, thus exposing their fellow-writers not only to the story itself, but also to the advisory notes of the director. And, finally, when the decision was made that these stories were worthy of publication, those finished pieces were passed on for professional editing and layout.

One can garner from the above that all of this endeavour on the part of our writers was about nothing if not hard work, assiduous application and total commitment. Nothing short of these could have yielded such a result. Hence, my admiration for these young Clare authors. They have honoured the trust placed in them by their parents, teachers, librarians and me, and, in having done so, they have delivered selflessly and gloriously on the back of that trust. Up the Banner!

Huge thanks are due to the teachers of English and the librarians in each of the following: St. Patrick's Comprehensive School, Shannon; St. Caimin's Community School, Shannon; Kilrush Community School; St. Joseph's Community College, Kilkee; Ennistymon Vocational School; Scoil Mhuire, Ennistymon; and Meánscoil na mBráithre, CBS Ennistymon. Without their commitment and enthusiasm we would not have had our participants. Similarly, to the librarians and staff of our host libraries in Shannon, Kilrush and Ennistymon: the céad míle fáilte, the courtesy extended, the respect and hospitality given to our young writers and to me surpasses any that I have encountered in my 20 years of doing such work. These libraries are the literary lifeblood of the communities they serve – and they, by any standards, serve extremely well.

A particular thanks is due to you, the parents of these marvellous young people, for having trusted your sons' and daughters' creative talents to me. I have already said that they have served you well in that trust, but it equally warrants saying that *you too* have served *them* well in having responded positively to this opportunity that came their way. What ambassadors they have proven to be for you!

Earlier in this piece, I alluded to a number of visionary people being at the helm of the ship that has been this long endeavour, and it would be remiss of me not to say a little of them here. Courage and determination are qualities that are much needed in these straitened times, and they are the very qualities displayed by Helen Walsh, Clare County Librarian, since the inception of this course. Helen's commitment to the community she serves, along with her resolve that this opportunity should be extended to as many of County Clare's second-level students as possible, was the catalyst that drove what was to be initially a once-off course on into a second year, then on again into a third. She has my huge regard and is equally deserving of the regard of those whom she has served here. Clare County Arts Officer, Siobhán Mulcahy, showed equal commitment to this project and, at a time when another might have shirked from doing so, she stretched her office's limited resources to part-fund this effort, not flinching when the prospect of a second, and yet again, a third course was mentioned. And to MÓINÍN, of which I am a founder member, and more particularly to Ailsa Ellis, I extend my great regard and thanks. Without Ailsa's work of filing and documentation, and most particularly her computer formatting skills, I could never have done my end of the work.

All of which takes me to Patricia Fitzgerald, Executive Librarian for Children's and Teenage Literature – the one who, in the quietest, yet most efficient of ways has held all the strands of things together, the one for whom nothing has been too much trouble in administering this project. I have previously described Patricia as the pulse – the heartbeat – of all the work conducted in the course of three years of endeavour. She has been that and more. Nothing I can say or write can sufficiently express my gratitude to her. And so, Patricia, a sincere and simple thanks to you on a job that, from start to finish, has been so very well done.

And finally, to our young writers: my heartfelt thanks to you for having allowed me into your worlds, for your commitment, your hard work, your sense of seriousness and fun, your kindness and your sharing of your immense talents. It has been an absolute joy for me to have been around you. You are the Flyers of the Banner. You are the lights of our future. Your creative gifts may well be what sees us all through the austerity of these times. Breathe your light, your hope, your youthfulness out onto the world, and always remember that the marvellous talents you have been given are simply gifts. They are yours to use for the betterment of this world. *Beannacht libh i gcónaí.*

**Ré Ó Laighléis**
*Writer & Course Director*

# No Parking

## *Oisín Bates*

NO PARKING DAY OR NIGHT. The sign on the battered garage door, spelt out in bold block capitals, gave a clear message. Even if John had owned a car, it never would have crossed his mind to park it in front of old Mr. Garrathy's garage. John didn't know many eleven year-olds with cars, and besides, even if he did own one, he was sure his mother wouldn't approve. The illegal parking of cars had never been high on John's list of priorities. His interest lay instead with the hidden treasures behind the large wooden doors.

John had lived on the same street for almost ten years. Quite a credible achievement, given his tender age. More remarkable was the fact that, in all his years of residency, he had never so much as stolen a glance inside the heavy wooden doors that blocked the outside world from the unimaginable curiosities of old Garrathy's garage. It was widely accepted by most eleven year-olds of the area that Mr. Garrathy owned an old car – 'possibly a Ford', as one thoroughly nagged mother once divulged – to which, it was believed, he devoted his every Sunday, tinkering away. In the midst of this solid evidence, the secretive world had become an urban legend of sorts. Reluctant to accept the slightly bland reality, many children had concocted elaborate theories, some more suited to James Bond films than to anonymous suburban cul-de-sacs. Eager to capitalise on their children's fascination, most mothers joked that Old Garrathy actively interned children who didn't finish their broccoli. For want of a better explanation, John had gradually taken this obscure theory as truth.

During those long summer evenings, John had often taken to sitting patiently opposite the perpetually closed doors, but to no avail. Old Garrathy consistently proved himself an extremely elusive character. Perhaps, John would sometimes muse, he was a retired film star, or maybe – just maybe – an international criminal mastermind, in exile from foreign police. Whatever his reason for cooping himself within his secluded house may have been, he surely didn't get out much.

Mr. Garrathy's humble abode sat neatly nestled into a secluded corner at the end of the lane, the large garage doors backing onto the narrow, winding laneway which wound steadily towards a junction and the open roads beyond. John's house itself was but a stone's throw up the lane. From his upstairs bedroom window, John could view a small portion of the doors and the leaf-swept lane before it. His view was greatly impaired by the ancient drooping chestnut trees that lined the roadway. Each tree stood motionless, not unlike a sentry guarding its respective gateway. The long branches drooped over the lane, showering a confetti of golden leaves down upon the roadway below, as long summer evenings gave way to a lazy autumn twilight.

It was from this very window that, one Sunday evening, he caught a glimpse of those much-considered doors swinging ajar in the breeze. Seizing the moment, John rushed downstairs. Flinging on his shoes and pausing only to snatch his father's camera from the kitchen counter, he burst out the back door. It would be foolish, John thought, to let an opportunity like this go to waste. God knows when he'd ever get a second glance through those doors.

Galloping past his immediate neighbour's gates, John slowed to a virtual standstill as he approached the open doors, the excitement of what he might see overcoming the fear of getting caught. Peering cautiously through the opening, there was neither sight nor light of Old Garrathy to be seen. Seizing the opportunity, John crept through the open doors. Battered shelves lined the walls, groaning under the weight of a hundred cardboard boxes. Countless oily gears lay on the ground, scattered upon oilcloths.

Any free wall space was occupied by posters of vintage cars – a whole section dedicated to Monte Carlo rallies of years gone by. A workbench sat in the far corner of the room. Grilles and badges sat upon its rough wooden surface, all coated in shining chrome, all without a single blemish.

Amongst all this stood an old car, its shining bodywork glimmering under the soft glow of the overhead lighting. Every fixture and fitting was meticulously restored, its shining chrome complementing the olive green paint of the body. An odd, nostalgic shade – the type you wouldn't really find on modern cars. Standing amid all this, John somehow felt a strange sense of anticlimax. Where were the cages for the troublesome children? Or the crates of broccoli? Then John remembered the camera. Facing the grille, he aimed the camera steadily at the gleaming body. He couldn't but admire the shining car, as a bar of daylight crept through the open door and danced upon the gleaming bonnet. And, just as he pressed to take the photo, John heard the creaking of the large doors opening wide behind him. Turning timidly, he could feel the blood slowly draining from his body.

"Well, if it isn't wee John Fitzgerald! Christ, I haven't seen you in years."

A sense of nausea swept over John and his eyes jumped to meet those of the old man, and then back to the car.

"Nice car, isn't she? Ford Anglia. Bought her new, kept her since. I take her out the country roads once a month at dawn, but sure you'd still be in bed."

John stood silently. It was, if ever silence could be so described, an enlightened silence.

"Look at you, you must be starving! Come on into the house. The wife's making broccoli."

# Gone

## *Tara Mallon*

AS EMILY BOYLE drifted into sleep, she was oblivious to her mother, Brenda, awakening in the next room. Brenda was covered in a cold sweat. Her heart was pounding. She sat upright in the bed and struggled to catch her breath. It was the sixth night in a row that she had found herself rudely awoken from her dreams. The sixth night that she lay awake waiting for her daughter's familiar footsteps coming down the hall. So far, the footsteps hadn't come.

Brenda got out of bed and went downstairs to put the kettle on. She had no desire for tea, but the ritual seemed to give her fleeting comfort. As the kettle boiled, she looked at the pictures hanging around the kitchen. Pictures of herself, her husband Matthew and their twin children, Emily and Shauna, on holiday a few years ago in Croatia. Others of her two girls celebrating various birthdays over the years. Then pictures of them in their primary school uniforms. She focused on one that was taken about twelve years ago, when the girls were just five years old. Emily looked uncomfortable and camera shy, while Shauna, always the more outgoing of the two, smiled and posed. Brenda had always thought this picture summed the twins up perfectly.

She felt tears running down her cheeks as she looked at her beautiful girls with their white blonde hair, their identical blue eyes. To this day, she and Matt were the only ones capable of telling the two apart. She smiled fondly as she thought of the many tricks the girls had played on teachers and friends since they were no age. Shauna was always the ringleader, of course. Emily, the more academic of the two, was sensible and extraordinarily good in school, rarely causing trouble. Shauna, on the other hand, was rarely out of trouble. She was the charming one, witty and sociable. The two were practically inseparable – always had been.

Brenda was sitting on the floor now, her head pressed against the cupboards. She was crying so hard it felt as if her insides were going to split.

"Why me?" she asked herself aloud, again and again. What had she done to deserve the mental turmoil of a missing child? She wished and prayed for Shauna's safe return. She barely noticed Matt sitting down beside her and taking her in his arms.

It was Friday night last that Emily and Shauna had gone out to a local pub to celebrate the 18th birthday of one of their close friends, Patrick. Though only a week or so before the Leaving Cert results, and despite the girls being only 17, Brenda and Matt had decided to allow them go to the party. They knew Patrick well and they knew their girls were sensible enough to be home at a reasonable hour.

Emily was apprehensive about going out that night. Unlike her sister, she wasn't much of a drinker. Shauna had been drinking since she was 15, and although Emily always tagged along, she never joined in. She simply took on the role of looking after her sister and ensuring her parents didn't find out about her drinking.

But that night was different. Emily was dressed to kill, in the hopes of catching the eye of Patrick's best mate, Rob. She had been spotting him for a while, but he never seemed to notice her. Truth is she was never noticed because of her sister, despite their being identical. Shauna had the personality and the confidence around boys that Emily could only dream of. The girls separated straight away when they got to the party. Shauna made a beeline for a group of lads from the boys' school down the road and Emily went to Patrick to wish him a happy birthday.

"Alright, Em, where's your sister then, huh? I suppose she's too busy flirting to make time for the birthday boy!" he said, jokingly.

"Ah now, Pa, what did you expect? I'm the one you can depend on. Now don't you forget it, right!"

"Sure don't I know it! Em, you know Rob, don't you?"

And that was it – she was head over heels in love. They spent the whole night chatting away, getting to know each other, dancing and kissing. Emily couldn't wait to tell her sister how she had managed to get in with the best-looking guy in the pub! The whole thing just overwhelmed her. She even allowed herself to get a little bit drunk. She was having such a good time that she hadn't even taken stock of Shauna.

It was her mother's crying that woke Emily. It felt like she had just nodded off when she heard the sound of her mother sobbing from downstairs. She sat up in the bed and turned on the lamp, wincing as her eyes adjusted to the light. She looked around at the room – her room, Shauna's room, the room in which they'd laughed and cried together over the last 17 years. Everything seemed the same. Clothes scattered everywhere, make-up littering the dressing table, pictures and posters covering the walls. Everything was the same, yet something felt different. There was an emptiness. Emily felt like a stranger amongst the clothes and bits and bobs that she and Shauna shared. She looked over at her sister's empty bed and her heart ached in agony. The grief that she had felt over the last six days was unbearable. She hoped beyond hope that Shauna would come home soon. She wanted to cry, but she couldn't. Her parents had been crying almost non-stop for the last five days, after the realisation that Shauna might not come home. The Guards had been called the Saturday morning after the party, when Emily realised that her twin not only hadn't come home from the night before, but hadn't even been in contact. She had rung and texted her, but to no avail. Emily had got pretty drunk the night before and Rob had accompanied her in the taxi home. He was a lovely guy and had rung Emily a number of times over the last couple of days to see if she was OK. But the guilt she felt over spending the night with him, rather than looking after her sister would never subside.

It is the loud knock on the front door that disrupts her train of thought. It echoes through the house, as if banging off every surface. A glance at the clock: 4.43am. She steps out of bed and walks out on the landing. She makes her way towards the sound of the low voices, now coming from the living room below. Mother's voice. Father's voice. And then a younger voice. Shauna, she thinks. Yes, she thinks – she's home. Emily bounds down the stairs – her heart, her mind consumed by excitement. She rounds the banister, down the hallway and in the door of the living room. And there before her, her parents, cradled in each other's arms, sobbing, broken, shattered.

The young female Garda turns to Emily. "I'm sorry, love. It's …"

# The Death Penalty

*Jim Downes*

RODRIGO WAS HAUNTED by this one memory. A fluke! That's all it was, a fluke! Pure bad luck. Another six inches and the ball would have been in, he thought, as he pushed his hands into the sinkful of water and splashed his burning face. Then, the images of the LCD screen high up in the stadium flashed to mind, the ball ricocheting off the bar and bouncing slowly over the end-line. Everything in slow and painful motion. The echoing memory of the opposition fans' cries mounted, as though still filling his ears. Then, out of the mania, his mind going at a hundred miles an hour, he reached for the cabinet over the sink and located the Panadol. Relief for now, he thought.

The bus journey to the stadium was both unnerving and exciting. Fans filled the streets, singing and cheering. More than anything, it was the clear Kop roar that got the nerves tingling. But he tired quickly of this carnival-like frenzy and resorted to his iPod. First were the soft rhythmic sounds of Jamaican Bob Marley, then the inspiring rock anthems of Bruce Springstein – all easing him into a relative remove.

Inside the dressing room, a general sense of apprehension mounted. There was the non-purpose shaking of legs, the conventional sprints back and forth between the bathrooms, and much else. Last minute calls from physios for massages rang around the tension-filled changing room. The squeaking of ankle tape jarred on players' minds. The heart-wrenching speech of Captain Gavin Malone and a passionate call to arms by the Gaffer, Frank McIntyre, all served to get the blood racing in their veins.

Then, the knock on the door by the TV official really made anxiety kick in. And, in no time, the opposing teams found themselves in the middle of the stadium, surrounded by a sea of strong and sweeping colour. Rodrigo had never experienced anything like this before and he swelled with excitement as the names were called out. Roars accompanied the announcements, but, in the young kid's case there was a mixture of cheers and boos.

Rodrigo got his first touch and all the nerves were gone. Adrenaline kicked in, moves were made and tackles skipped, all rendering the young man oblivious to the passage of time. And, in what appeared to be no time at all, it was the 87th minute mark. The crowd's attention increasingly shifted between the action and the scoreboard. Still scoreless, and there were only two clear-cut chances in the game, both of which fell to the opposition.

Not again, feared Rodrigo. I'm not letting this pass me by again, he thought, as he sprinted after what seemed a lost cause. "I'm going to win this," he said aloud.

It was a head-to-head chase between the dynamic youngster and the opposition's tough and unsparing centre-half. Rodrigo quickly cut inside, but it was too late. Bang!! He was hit low and venomously.

Suddenly, the vast majority of Liverpool's players ran to protest to the referee. But the decision was already made. The referee's hand hovered over the penalty spot. Loud choruses of 'You'll Never Walk Alone' rang around the stadium. The overhead camera zoomed in on Rodrigo, who was still receiving attention to his ankle injury. Whilst on the ground, he took a quick glance over towards the bench and to the Gaffer, then got the nod: he was taking the penalty.

"This is your chance to prove everyone wrong," said an out-of-breath Gavin Malone, who had made the trip up from centre-half to help Rodrigo back onto his feet. "We believe in you, mate."

The ball was on the white spot and the goalkeeper and referee were in position. Rodrigo took his customary steps back – his usual pattern. As he eyed the goalie, the images of last week's

# Truth

## *Dearbhla Edwards-Murphy*

DAYS AND WEEKS progressed into months, but the loneliness of widowhood lingered. Though the funeral and burial had passed, the pain was still as excruciating as ever. He had left her. He needed a way out. Doubt had whirled around in Sharon's head, forcing her into deep depression.

Even the most minuscule of an everyday task seemed daunting to Sharon now. She'd been putting off going to the supermarket. But now that everything had calmed down and her sister was reaching the final stages of pregnancy, she became less available to do much of the running for her. Sharon needed to get back to living independently. But she couldn't help but dwell on the past.

Sharon, not in the best state due to her prolonged lack of appetite, strolled down the cereal aisle. Coco Pops seemed like a good choice. Not the most nutritious, but chocolate was a comforting food. Exactly what she needed. She stopped mid-reach. If she wouldn't look after herself, then who would? The darkly clad young woman steered herself past the biscuit and cakes section that, in all her 29 years, had never looked so tempting. Not even after her parents sustained fatal head injuries in a car collision, more than a decade and a half ago, had she tried this hard to resist a binge diet.

Everywhere she turned, reminders of young Garda Kate O'Brien came flooding back to her. The way she clutched her mug tightly in her hands, or how time apparently stood still as she tried to comprehend the words: *'Your husband is dead. Evidence suggests suicide'*. These memories etched themselves into Sharon's brain, refusing to ever be forgotten.

The sight of exotic fruit triggered a further series of painful twists in Sharon's stomach, as she recalled their Hawaiian getaway at Easter. Jonathan seemed happy during the walks on countless beautiful beaches, their attempt at surfing and a few visits to volcano national parks. Had she ignored signs of his psychological distress? Sharon did a U-turn out of the fruit and veg aisle. Maybe Coco Pops weren't such a bad idea.

The colourful 'Back 2 School' advertising was an unwelcome reminder to Sharon of her imminent return to the classroom. She wasn't rejoicing at the thought of having to encourage a toddler out from under a table or intervening in play-dough fights. Least of all, watching doting parents playing happy couples, while dropping their little terrors to school – the babysitting institution. At least it would distract her from … No, grocery shopping is too risky. Coco Pops aren't worth this, Sharon thought.

Day rolled into night, while grief became anger. 'How could he do this to me?' she asked herself, unsure of how much more of it she could take.

Sharon descended the final two steps of the stairs, scooped up the envelopes on the hallway floor and flicked through the letters.

"Bill, bill, bill …" she began to murmur, before trailing off.

There was a letter there addressed to Jonathan.

"Is this some kind of sick joke?" she quipped aloud, as she tore open the envelope and unfolded the letter. Sharon was well aware that opening someone else's mail was a big no-no, but surely this didn't apply to the deceased. Her eyes widened, her face portraying shock. It was a notice from a gambling website, online poker and betting. Jonathan didn't gamble. Well, at least not anymore. He'd had a few serious problems a few years back. Drink, drugs, you name it, but he had promised he'd never relapse into his woeful teenage state. Must be a mistake, Sharon thought, as she tore the paper to shreds.

Reunited classmates greeted each other warmly at the school gate, as Sharon passed in brisk, long strides, making her way to the staff room. The chatter of fellow-teachers lightened her mood, or perhaps it was because she was no longer wearing mourning clothes. In their place was one of her usual work outfits, even if it was one of the least brightly coloured of them. The teachers gingerly tried to include her in the conversation, something for which she was grateful.

By break-time Sharon had had her fair share of toddlers' tantrums. The relief of fresh air while patrolling the schoolyard helped clear her head. Unexpectedly, her mind's wandering was interrupted by a whine.

"Miss, Miss! Sheanie kicked the ball into the car park again."

Sharon sighed and dutifully abandoned her post by the gate to make her way to the school car park. In the distance, she noticed a man suspiciously hovering around the entrance. Now, more apprehensive in her approach, she slowed, but paid acute attention to the movement of the figure. The baggy apparel and large sunglasses worn by the bulky, hooded stranger made Sharon feel more unsettled. In a dozen more steps she'd be there. Suddenly, the man pulled off his sunglasses.

"Heya, Shar! Miss me?" A scarily familiar smile flashed across his face. *His* face! Jonathan's face! Surprise. Anger. Disbelief. An unsettling mixture of emotions seized Sharon's mind. But somehow, externally, she managed to compose herself, to keep her voice calm.

"Jonathan?" she said. Jonathan moved closer and cupped her face in his hands, drawing her towards him.

"I know, love, I know. But I came back for you."

Sharon stared into his eyes and alarm bells sounded.

"I'm sorry. I messed up, got involved with the wrong people." He stroked her hair. This was pushing it too far, but Sharon hesitated to pull away from his embrace. Nonetheless, an inner instinct told her to tread carefully. Something about the man she'd married wasn't quite right. He was not the man she'd thought him to be.

"I'm so sorry," Jonathan whispered.

"I'm sorry too," said Sharon, as she drew back from him.

# Release

## *Michael McInerney*

MRS. LANGLEY TURNED to see David slowly making his way towards the classroom door.

"Is everything OK, David?"

David started, almost as though he had been woken from a deep sleep.

"Em- e- em, y- y- yes, I'm fine thanks, just a b- bit tired," he stuttered, continuing towards the door. Mrs. Langley noticed how pale the poor boy looked. David exited the door with his eyes lowered. Once outside the school, he looked up and saw John waiting.

"Friday afternoon at last!" John commented. "Not a bad week now," he said in his usual carefree fashion. Oh, how David envied him.

"T- t- twas alright, I s'ppose."

"Any plans for the weekend?" asked John.

"Ehh, no, I don't think so." David shot a furtive look at his comrade as he said this. John was looking at him in that way he always did when he was about to ask David to some party or other.

"Sure, Skippy is having his party tonight. Why don't you call over? It's on around 8 o'clock. Might get yourself a bit of leg!"

John's eyes twinkled mischievously. Visions of disco scenes flashed through David's head. Dad would never let him go. But he could sneak out. But then ... Punishment.

"I'll see. I'm not t- t- too sure i- i- if I can go yet."

"Up to yourself, man. Everyone's going. Johnny, Pepe, Sparky and the lads. It'll be mad craic. Anyways, talk to ya later."

After a complicated sequence of hi-fives and handshakes, the two boys parted ways and headed for their respective destinations.

"I'm home," said David, closing the door behind him and dropping his bag in the hall. He peered into the kitchen. His mother was sitting at the table with a distant look in her eyes.

"Mom? I'm home," David said again, this time a little louder.

His mother slowly turned her head and nodded. She stood up gingerly and tottered towards David. The bruising on her arm was plain to see.

"S- so, how are you f- f- feeling today, Mom?"

"I'm fine," his Mom whispered, as though speech hurt. And David knew why that was so.

"Mom, we have to stop him. If we r- r- ring the Guards, t- t- they will sort it out." His mother looked up, terror in her eyes.

"No, I'm fine I said. It's just some light bruising. I'm fine. There is no need to involve the Guards."

"B- b- but what about your ribs?" stuttered David. 'Why do I bloody stutter like this?' he mused. 'He isn't even here. There is nothing for me to worry about'.

"I said I'm fine. Now leave it, son," his Mom said, giving him a look that closed the conversation. David thought it better not to push it at this point. He smiled a weak, forced smile and headed up to his room.

The clock chimed 8 o'clock. David slowly walked down the stairs. He had listened through the door all evening as his Mom and Father had fought again. It had been the same story as the many other nights. Mom screaming in pain. Father laughing. A thousand thoughts flitted through David's brain. 'I can't block it out anymore', he thought. 'I have to get out. He can't stop me. Can he?'

He reached the bottom step and slipped into the sitting room. His Dad was seated in the armchair, his mother on the couch, just across from him. Looking at them, you would swear they were a normal couple. Except for the fresh bruising on his mother's face.

David's father looked up, immediately taking in David's 'going out' shirt, jeans and gelled-up hair.

"Going somewhere, son?" His voice was level, almost casual. But his steel, grey eyes betrayed him. David felt his pulse quicken. Instantly, his hands felt sweaty. If he turned away now and changed, there would be no trouble. For today. But what about tomorrow? What about the weeks, the months, the years ahead?

"Em, I- I- I'm going to Skippy's. H- h- h- he is having a party."

"Did you ask if you could go?" There was threat in his father's voice. David could feel the blood course through his body. Faster, faster. 'Father is angry now', thought David. 'Oh God, what have I done this time?'

"Ehh- ehh, n- n- n ..."

"Ah, stop bloody stuttering like a fool!"

David felt his face redden at this. 'How dare he rebuke me like this', thought David, 'when he is the reason for the bloody thing'.

Then, the usual explosion "Well, did you ask if you could go?"

'Oh God! He is standing up now'.

David glanced at his mother. She turned away. They both knew what was coming. His father rushed forward and pushed David.

"Don't touch me," the youngster rasped.

"What did you say?"

"Don't touch me," retorted David, and this time his defiance was even stronger, stutter nowhere to be heard. "I'll call the Guards."

With that, David's father spun around to look at his wife. "Did you know about this party? Eh? Did you give him these notions about the Guards?" David's mother just whimpered. "Answer me, you whore." He was shaking with anger.

'I've got to stop him', thought David. Then, impulsively, he grabbed his father by the shoulder. But his father's reaction was instantaneous. Before David knew what had happened, he was swished around and his arm was twisted upwards into that hollow between his shoulder blades. The pain! Tears welled up in the teenager's eyes, but he held them back. Then he stared

16

defiantly at his father. His father stared back threateningly, menacingly, intent on breaking his son's resistance. But then David wrenched his arm from his father's grip. He didn't care what would happen now. He eyed his father hard, then headed towards the front door.

"I am going to Skippy's party, whether you like it or not. I'll be back around 12."

"You get back here now, laddie, or you *know* what's going to happen."

David stopped and turned back momentarily. "Nothing is going to happen," he said defiantly. And, with that, he exited and drew the door behind him.

Before he reached the front gate, David heard his mother's fear-filled wail. He leaned up against the garden hedge and took his mobile from his pocket. The light of the screen reflected on his drawn face as he scrolled down to find the number of the local Garda Station.

# The Incident

## *Sabrina Vaughan*

A COLD MONDAY MORNING. Claire knew that it was time. Her father would trundle overhead and come hunt her out of her bedroom. But this time was different. She knew she had to get up, but she waited. And, as she waited, she could hear a loud, annoying, beeping sound from across the room.

"Just two more minutes," she grumbled.

"Claire, get up," her father barked, with that croaky voice of his. Claire groaned.

"Come on, the car is frozen, so you'll have to walk to the bus."

Claire suddenly rolled in her unmade heap of a bed. "*Me?*" she said, as if to suggest that it could possibly be someone else.

"Well, it's hardly likely that *I'm* going to go," said her father, chirpily.

Claire did not want to go to school that morning, knowing what would await her at the gates. She put on her uniform and took her money off the kitchen table. She grabbed her bag, raced out the door and power-walked up the road to catch her only transport for the ten-mile journey to school.

Claire hated everything about school. Teachers, the work, the classrooms, even her fellow-pupils. Particularly her fellow-pupils. She couldn't take it any more. She couldn't stand their whispering behind her back. Arriving at the school, she could see her classmates waiting outside the gate, ready to go to PE. Her friend James was there, along with the rest of the boys.

"Hey, Claire!" said James, as she walked up the hill. "How have you been?" Before she could answer, the PE instructor pointed to the school, indicating that she should get a move on. She sighed and walked inside to drop off her school bag.

Once upstairs, she dropped her bag in the girls' bathroom and, as she threw her jacket into her open, banged-up locker, two other girls entered. One was pretty, tall and blonde. The second girl was small and pudgy, but strong.

"Let's show her what you can do," whispered the tall one, Jessica, to her slave.

Jessica grabbed Claire, swinging her around and cupping her hand across her mouth. At the same time, the pudgy girl stomped aggressively towards her, driving her oversized fist up into Claire's ribs. Claire squealed in pain. The slave did it again and again until the first tear came from Claire's eye and she lay helplessly on the floor.

"If you ever so much as look, let alone speak to my boyfriend again," said Jessica, "I'll get Jenny to pay you another little visit, you cow."

She was found an hour later by one of the teachers who was on her way to the toilet. Her parents and all the teachers had questioned her about the incident, but she gave no answer. Any time anyone questioned her, she froze and thought of what Jessica had said to her about Jenny paying another visit.

Jenny had been leering intimidatingly at Claire throughout the week. Apart from the beating incident, Claire didn't even know this Jessica, let alone the fact that she had a boyfriend. She hadn't a clue what she had done to deserve this. But she knew that she couldn't take it any longer. She had to talk to someone, but to whom? Who could she tell who wouldn't judge her, who would take her side?

Perchance, some eight or nine days after the beating, she came across a sticker on the back of the bathroom door. She had been spending a lot of her time in the bathroom, hiding from Jessica and Jenny: *Confidential Services for Social and Domestic Abuse – violence, physical, sexual, emotional, etc.,* the sticker read. Claire scribbled the number on her sweaty palm.

That night Claire locked her door and sat on the bed. She had the number on a piece of paper in one hand and a phone in the other. She composed herself and pondered all that had happened. How Jenny had stomped towards her. How she had driven her oversized fist up into her ribs. How the threat of even more loomed heavily in the offing. With that, she flipped open the phone ...

# Armageddon

## *Jason Roche*

IT IS THE YEAR 2121. We find ourselves in post-apocalyptic times. No one really knows or cares about how the world ended anymore. In fact, the only thing of real concern to anyone is survival. In this troubled time there is a shortage of food, an extreme scarcity of clean water and you'd be killed on the spot for so much as a few drops of fuel …

But enough about that. Let me tell you about Chris, a wanderer just trying to survive, like everyone else. The one thing about Chris is that he never leaves anyone behind.

Gunfire breaks out! Outnumbered six to one.

"There aren't enough of these psychos to stop me," says Chris, as he kills two of them with his handgun. Suddenly, while he is taking cover, an active grenade lands beside him. With a surge of adrenaline, he kicks the grenade back at the marauders, killing the rest of them. "That's what they get for attacking me," he quips. Then he scavenges what he can from the bodies and heads off on the road again.

A sudden stop. 'How the hell can I be out of gas?' he asks himself. When he gets out, he instantly sees the trail of fuel from his now-punctured gas tank. Stooping to investigate, there, lodged in the metal tank, he sees a bullet from the previous fire fight, which had taken place some fifty miles away. Stranded, he gathers up his equipment and continues down the sun-parched highway.

After walking two miles or so, he encounters a person who is dying of thirst and begging for water. Chris, against all survival instincts, gives him his last bottle of water. The beggar thanks him sincerely and Chris then continues walking.

Three days in this heat without food or water makes him weary and, after a few more hours of wandering in the desert, he stumbles across an oasis. He drinks as much as he needs and fills up his containers with water. Energy restored now, he resumes his journey.

Eventually, he comes across a peculiar town that was built in post-apocalyptic times. He enters the town, speaks with the mayor and asks for refuge.

"What makes you think you're deserving of refuge in this town? You'll have to do somethin' to prove your worth."

"Okay, what do you want?"

After much negotiation, the mayor agrees that he can live there if he takes care of a marauder problem the town has been having.

In the town, Chris encounters a cocky sharpshooter named Mack.

"Hey, are you some kind of wanderer?" asks Mack.

"Name's Chris."

"Aren't you the one who's been hunting down marauders? I hear you agreed to take out Bludge and his crew."

"What's it to you?"

"Well, I wanna help you do it."

"Why?"

"Because that asshole Bludge killed my family."

"Fair enough, I'm not going to stop you."

"Thanks, Chris."

The two of them team up and head out to the marauder camp. Mack provides sniper cover, while Chris clears the camp from room to room. Eventually, when all the marauders are dead, Chris lets his guard down and is pinned to the wall by an arrow fired by Bludge.

"I'm gonna kill the stupid wastelanders that are in my camp," says Bludge.

He then picks up an axe and charges at Chris, but Mack shoots the axe out of his hand. Chris points his gun at the leader of the marauders, but Bludge hits him with a hammer and takes the gun off him. Bludge shoots the gun at Mack and then he turns to shoot Chris, only to see nothing before him.

"Where's that other bastard gone? He was here a minute ago."

Confused, he turns around and Chris stabs Bludge in the head. "I'm sick of this shit," he says.

Chris pulls the arrow out of his stomach, then goes to check on Mack, who, though badly wounded, is still alive.

"You okay, Mack?"

"I'll be fine."

"Hang on. I'll get you to a doctor."

Chris picks him up and carries him three miles to the nearest doctor. Job done, duty delivered upon, Chris then finally settles down.

# An Oíche

## *Rebecca Austin*

THE MUSIC STARTS TO PLAY. It is loud, with a faint crackling sound that fills the whole rural dance hall. The speakers blare traditional Irish songs that have been played at so many other Irish college céilís, like the one at which Elizabeth finds herself. The floorboards groan under the weight of some two hundred people dancing to the Walls of Limerick along with her. Fiachra and Elizabeth stand awkwardly next to each other, their clammy hands clasped in each other's, as they move to the beat. She's glad that they are so close to the speakers. It makes conversation almost impossible. As the dance continues, they proceed down the hall, passing others they know. Boys from his house wink and nod, gesturing towards Elizabeth. Girls from her house giggle and point in their direction. Why is it that in the Gaeltacht nothing is ever a secret? The dance ends and Fiachra and Elizabeth exchange a few words.

The bus journey home is one that Elizabeth could nearly do in her sleep at this point. She lets herself be lead to the bus by the other girls in her house.

"*Suigh in aice liomsa,*" Kate calls out, as Elizabeth steps onto the bus.

"*Bhuel, conas atá tú, Kate? Aon scéal?*"

"Never mind that, Elizabeth. I heard tonight that Siobhán has a thing for Fiachra. Watch your step around her."

"What! Are you serious? Any excuse she has now she's going to kill me!"

Elizabeth isn't up for much now. She is dreading getting back to the house. Siobhán will most likely give her a hard time about something or other. Probably something small, like the cleaning of the plates after dinner. But at least there is something to look forward to tonight: the teachers will be coming around to all the houses to give the students their phones so that they can call home.

"*Tá carr an mhúinteora ag teacht*," comes a high-pitched screech from another room. Elizabeth abandons her letter, runs downstairs with the rest of the girls and gets her phone from the teacher. As she walks outside she turns it on. The old polysonic sound fills the evening air. She dials the familiar home number and is greeted by her mother.

"Hello?"

"Hi, Mom, it's me."

"Elizabeth! It's great to hear from you. I've missed you so much! It's so quiet here without you. How are you getting on?"

Elizabeth pauses and thinks. She can't tell her Mom what a horrible time she is having, how Siobhán, her Cinnire Tí, is so nasty to her, how all she wants is to go home.

"Are you still there?" her mother asks, interrupting her daughter's train of thought.

"It's OK, I guess," says Elizabeth, her voice crackling as she starts to cry a little.

"Elizabeth, are you crying?"

"No, Mom. I just have a sore throat. Everything is fine."

"Well, if you're sure. Dad and I will be there to collect you on Sunday at 10 o'clock, and we can stop on the way home for a nice meal. It's hard to believe that you've been away for almost three weeks!"

"Yes, I know, Mom. I'm looking forward to that now. Will you bring my iPod with you?"

"Of course I will. So, is there any news there? Anything exciting happening? Any boyfriend?"

Elizabeth had been wondering what she would say if her mother were to ask her that this time. Well, technically speaking, Fiachra isn't really her boyfriend, so she wouldn't be lying to her mother. He's simply a boy that she likes.

"Well?" her mother's voice prompted, jarring her back to reality.

"No, Mom, no boyfriend. Look, I better go. The teacher is calling us."

"OK. It was lovely talking to you. We can't wait to see you on Sunday. Bye."

"Me too. Bye." And with that she hangs up.

As she walks back towards the front door of the house – the prison in which Siobhán can torment her – she wipes away her tears. Siobhán would slag her if she saw her crying. Now a thought replaces the tears and she begins to smile to herself. Tomorrow is the night-out for the cinnirí tí, and the tradition of playing pranks on them isn't lost on Elizabeth. This is her chance to pay back Siobhán.

As she reaches the top of the stairs and looks into her room, she sees a foot on her bed. Odd, she thinks. What's someone doing on her bed? She nears the door and there's Siobhán sitting on her bed, reading. What's she reading? She has never struck Elizabeth as the type that would read of her own free will. As Elizabeth draws even closer, she sees it is the letter that she had been writing to her friend Caoimhe back home. A private letter! What's she doing reading it? Elizabeth bursts in and snatches the letter from her.

"That's mine. What are you doing, Siobhán?"

"Reading," comes the smart, curt answer that one could only expect from Siobhán.

"I know you're reading, but that's my letter." She struggles to say it without starting to cry again.

"And a lovely letter it is, Liz. I didn't half know that you liked Fiachra that much. Don't worry, I'll have a word with him tomorrow." She smirks and begins to walk out.

"Don't you dare say anything to him, or to anyone!"

"I'll say whatever I want, bitch, and you won't stop me." And, with that, she turns on her heels and departs the room, leaving

Elizabeth speechless and hating her even more than she already does.

Elizabeth tosses and turns all night, unable to get any proper sleep. She wakes early and heads straight for the bathroom. Better to shower before everyone else wakes and starts fighting for 'first-in'. One small bathroom between ten, not to mention the family they are boarding with!

The day is a blur. She sees Siobhán talk to Fiachra, but she isn't all that bothered, now that she has calmed down. Tonight will finally be her chance to get her back and the best bit is that Siobhán won't know who pulled what pranks.

Once they are back in the house, they start setting up all the different pranks. Chilli powder on Siobhán's toothbrush, fake tan wipes instead of make-up remover, all her clothes stolen, nettles in her bed, the removal of the lightbulb and daubing Vaseline on any surfaces that Siobhán might touch. Yes, it's messy and they will all have to clean it up in the morning, but it's worth it. Anything to get her back is worth it.

Siobhán isn't going to be back till late. In fact, not till after 2am – well past curfew. So all the girls fall asleep, spent by the excitement of the day.

It is the early hours when Elizabeth awakens to the slamming of the door. Oh no, Siobhán is home and, by the sounds of it, she doesn't think the pranks are as funny as the pranksters do. And, just as that thought comes into her head, Elizabeth's bedroom door cracks open, spilling light onto the floor. Siobhán steps in, reaches for Elizabeth's bed and grabs her by the scruff of the neck, hauling her out of the bed and up to her level.

"Think you're so funny, don't you? You're dead!"

Elizabeth opens her mouth to let out a scream for help. But nothing comes. Again, an attempted scream, but still nothing.

Siobhán drags Elizabeth out the bedroom door, down the stairs and heads towards the front door. The Cinnire Tí then opens it without a sound and pushes the shoeless Elizabeth outside.

"Now, walk. We're going to the beach," hisses Siobhán in the darkness.

"But, but, but, why, Siobhán? Why so late?"

"Stop asking questions and just do it."

They walk, Elizabeth leading, Siobhán to the rear, pushing the younger girl every now and then. Running away is not an option. Anyway, there is nowhere to go. And soon the tarmac merges with a grainy, sandy-textured surface.

"Hello?" Siobhán calls out into the night.

A grunt of sorts comes in reply, then two figures come into view. Elizabeth can only make out one of them. It's Fiachra. He's shoeless too. She doesn't know whether to be worried or be relieved at this.

"Ye two think you're so funny, don't you?" says the voice of the unknown male.

"Well, you're here now, barefooted, and with no way back – not that that would be much good to you, even if you did know the way," says Siobhán. And, with that, Siobhán and the other figure flee off into the distance, laughing at the sick joke.

As Elizabeth turns to Fiachra, they look down at each other's feet and what had been sleet begins to turn to heavy rain.

# The Way of War

## *Samuel Kenyon*

THE FLARE ARCHED through the air, casting a harsh red light over the drab landscape, which was pitted with holes from artillery barrages. Bodies were strewn generously on the space between the two sets of trenches. Most troopers had their heads down, grabbing vital hours of sleep, with a minimal watch posted. None but a certain Frederick Adams watched the flare trace its arc through the cloudy night sky. He couldn't sleep because he had, this very afternoon, received a letter from his family in America. They had also sent him a present – a scope for his rifle. He had fitted it immediately and, on sudden impulse, he had grabbed the gun and decided to try it out. The trench was a bit deeper than a man was tall, so there were low wooden platforms for the men to stand on. Fred stepped up onto one such platform, but the recent rains had churned the trenches into a sea of mud, so that the wood underfoot was treacherously slippery. He grabbed the earth above the trench for support. That was his mistake.

Across in the enemy trench, the German sharpshooter, Friedrich van Haarken, eye pressed keenly against the scope of his rifle, noticed movement. A hand grappled with the sparse vegetation, then a full arm came into view. He grinned maliciously. Fool! Quick movements attracted attention. Slow and steady was the trick. He drew a bead on the arm and smirked. He hadn't missed yet and to Friedrich this was an easy target, with the flare illuminating it. He squeezed the trigger.

Fred just had his head over the top of the trench when he heard the shot. Almost simultaneously he was thrown back – down, down, down into the cold mud. He saw his mother – old, white-haired. Was she never to know what had become of him?

It started raining. A burning fire ran up his arm. The pain was excruciating. Blood leaked through his fingers as he clutched the wound. The bullet had entered between his elbow and shoulder. He ripped off a piece of the blood-soaked sleeve and examined the injury. The bullet had gone straight through, rather than lodging in the bone. This was good, but it was still a serious injury. He rummaged at his waistband and located the first-aid kit on his belt. He managed to wrap a clean piece of cloth around the wound and give himself a shot of morphine. Relief was all but instantaneous. Though the pain hadn't fully gone away, it had at least been dulled. Then, suddenly, he decided to give that damned German a taste of his own medicine. He stood up unsteadily.

In the far trench, Friedrich gnawed on a piece of hardtack and reflected on his recent sniping. He was good at it, cold, malicious, and he enjoyed making people suffer. Maybe, he thought, when this was all over, he would hire himself out. A good idea. A hired assassin. He looked towards the American trench again, totally unsuspecting. How much pain that idiotic American sod must be feeling!. How much ... Wait! What was that? Too late he saw the danger. Too slow to move before the bullet pierced his chest.

In the American trench, Fred had watched the German straighten, then fall back into the hole. The American climbed back down into his own trench. He looked at his wound. He might lose some of the nerves in his hand, or even die, he thought. He smiled grimly.

In the German trench, a hand twitched.

# Breaking Focus

## *Áine O'Halloran*

"IS THAT WHAT YOU'RE SAYING, Danielle, is it? That you can't do this anymore?"

I carefully closed my eyes and tried to breath slowly. Calm, Danielle, now is not the right time. Then again, it's never the right time for this, I told myself, as I began recalling every second prime number. I was consciously aware of Gina talking constantly as numbers ran through my head … 3 … 7 … 13 …

"Well?" Gina demanded, looking more angry than I'd ever seen her in our seven years of friendship. But I couldn't break my focus, not this close to the end. Keep going, I told myself. Then things won't get worse. Who knows if you stop.

As Gina continued to rant and rave, I couldn't stop a single tear trickling slowly down my face. I just kept counting. Once I had finished, I looked up to see her staring down at me, tapping her foot angrily.

"An explanation might be nice, please?" she said, her words cutting through me like a knife.

"It's complicated," I began. "My school work is piling up and my parents want me to study more," I finished, lamely.

"That's it? That's the reason you're throwing away all we've worked for. All your talent, not to mention your bandmates and your friends?"

I wanted to say no, that it wasn't even the real reason, but I knew I could never tell Gina the truth. She would never understand. Even my parents still don't understand, no matter how hard they try. They can never understand why I must tap the kitchen table before sitting down or how I count the tiles on the hall floor as many times as it takes to feel right before even leaving the house.

I was diagnosed with Obsessive Compulsive Disorder – OCD – when I was 12 years old, but it began years before, when I was nine. Most cases of OCD begin in childhood and mine was no exception. I first noticed it one day when I was in my grandparents' house in Dundrum and I suddenly felt an urge to count all the ornaments on their mantelpiece, from right to left. I repeated it a total of fifteen times, counting those porcelain cocker spaniel puppies until it felt better. Right-to-left, then left-to-right, then right-to-left again. I wasn't even conscious of my grandmother watching me intently as I counted. What I didn't know at the time was that she had taken my mother aside afterwards and told her what she had seen me doing. I later learned that her father had counted and performed rituals just like she had seen me do that day. She had recognised it for what it was, and my mother took me to our local doctor the very next day.

As I walked into the surgery, I looked at the drab orange walls and took in the hard modern chairs that were lining the surgery waiting room. The secretary was a stern-looking woman, with greasy grey hair tied back in a bun, which made her look even more severe and dangerous than ever. Her expression and gruff manner succeeded in making me more nervous and, out of nowhere, I got this overwhelming urge to count prime numbers, feeling that, if I didn't, then things could go horribly wrong. I don't know why, but I just sensed that something terrible would happen if I didn't count and, no matter what, I couldn't shake off the irrational feeling. I tried to suppress it as long as I could, but I couldn't control it any longer.

Since I was diagnosed, my life had been turned upside down, controlled by the disease. I felt like I was disappearing, that the disease was eating away at who I was, slowly reducing me to a nervous wreck.

On my way home from my argument with Gina, I caught a passing glimpse of myself in the window of a River Island shop and barely recognised myself. The girl who stared back at me was pale – paler than I'd ever seen myself – and her face was thin and drawn. There were dark, purple bruise-like rings around her eyes and she looked as though she hadn't slept well, or even slept at all in weeks. I turned away from the window and, as I began the solitary walk home, I rummaged in my bag to find my earphones and iPod that I knew to be somewhere in my apparel. As the blaring guitar of Paramore bled from the earphones, I began to think on what I had just done. I walked, unthinkingly turning into Ludford Park, the housing estate next to mine. It had become more of a ritual than anything else, to call for my fellow-bandmate, Mark, who was also one of my closest friends. As I walked down the narrow pathway, lit by the soft glow of the lamps above me, I felt more hopeless than ever in my life. I felt like I couldn't take this anymore and I needed a distraction. Mark was the last person I wanted to talk to right then, but before I could even stop them, my feet had carried me to the brightly painted red door of his house. Luckily, Mark answered the door and, before I could say a word, he had closed it behind him and moved down to his garden wall, motioning that I should follow him.

"Gina just called," he said, quietly.

"Oh!" I could feel the questions already mounting in his head, in a line, each waiting its turn to be asked. I knew what the first question would be.

"Why did you do it? Why did you quit the band? We are so close to making it! We have a gig tomorrow night, Danielle."

I winced as he said that and could easily believe that the change that had occurred in me over the last few months was obvious to him. The pressures of school and work and now the band had all become too much, the stress building up into a frenzy of rituals, worse than I'd ever seen them before. And I thought I had hidden them well from everyone, that I had kept them out of sight. But my medication no longer worked and my doctor couldn't raise the dosage any higher because of my age.

"I couldn't take it anymore, Mark. You know how hard school is at the moment. And my parents are putting more and more pressure on me to do well. You know how important getting into college is for me!"

"But that's not it, Danielle. I know you. I know you've been really … well, let's say 'tense' lately. You've been doing weird things for a while now. Maybe not everyone can see it, but I can, and I'm seriously worried about you."

As he said those words, I could feel the bile rising in the back of my throat and my heart began to beat with such force that I thought it would shoot out of my chest. Oh God, no, how could he have noticed! I thought I'd been so careful to keep this secret. Things were going so badly wrong, I just wanted to turn and run before things could get any worse. I let out a nervous laugh in an effort to cover up my racing heartbeat.

"Nothing's going on. It's just some stuff I really have no control over."

No, I couldn't really be about to tell him! I couldn't! If I did, I knew he would be horrified by the rituals and the endless cycles, and I knew he could never really accept me, if he were to know the truth.

"What kind of stuff?"

He was like a detective now, gone into interrogation mode, and I knew he wouldn't drop it until he'd get the truth. Before I could stop myself, I began talking incessantly, telling everything – the whole story – until I felt completely drained, but strangely at ease. It was as though someone had turned on a tap and the whole story – stress and all that had built up – was let out in one gushing tidal wave.

"Wow! And you've kept this secret the whole time? From all of us? All of your friends?"

I felt my lungs tighten as he said this and I could sense his shock and astonishment as he tried to put words together in an attempt to keep the conversation going. I could feel myself willing him to understand, or at least accept it without horror or disgust.

"Yeah, well, I couldn't tell you. It's horrible, and most people I know completely misunderstand it and would never even begin to dream of what it feels like to suffer from it. So how horrified are you?" I barely whispered those last few words.

"Horrified! Why would I be horrified?"

I saw surprise in his face as he spoke, his eyebrows raised as if it was the most alien thing he had ever heard in his life.

"Because it's an illness. It can't be cured. It makes me do stupid, repetitive things that make no sense and I can never be normal because of it!" I was nearly sobbing now.

"Hey, it's OK, you *are* normal! Just because you have this doesn't make you any different. Like you said, it's an illness, remember? It doesn't make you any different to any other person."

As he said that, I began to see things differently. He was right. Just because I had an illness didn't mean I should let it take over my life. Like a cold or flu, I could control the symptoms and all I needed were the right tools.

From that moment on I began to fight back. I said goodnight to Mark as soon as I had convinced him I was OK. He no longer looked shocked, merely slightly amused that I would ever have thought that he would look at me any differently or judge me because I had told him. I started back towards my own house after fixing my earphones back in place. I noticed the moon creeping slowly over the Dublin Mountains. Its light filtered the darkness, turning the leaves and walls to silver and illuminating the houses. Somehow, it made the road home look more peaceful. I turned the key in the lock, slowly crept into the hallway and felt an instant ease as I tapped the door frame in the usual place three times.

# Justice

## *Joe Brown*

THE CRAB SCUTTLED along the sea bed. It was a decent crab, as crabs go. It had salvaged some good fish corpses to eat, hid itself rather well in the sand and wasn't a bad fighter. It was, if such a thing could be, a happy crab. So, when it was picked up rather abruptly by an enormous claw, it understandably had a small heart attack. When it finished having this near-death experience, it saw an enormous eye, then had another heart attack for good measure. It tried to pinch the claw, but the thing, despite being soft-shelled, was unyielding. The Eye studied the unfortunate crab, before apparently losing interest, dropping it just as abruptly as it had been picked up.

The crab lay upside down on the sea bed, shocked. It had been a good crab. It hadn't violated any Crab Laws, as far as it knew. It had observed the Three Daily Rituals of Crabbiness, which mainly consisted of fighting, eating and helping elderly crabs across dangerous currents. And yet *this* had happened. *This!* It had been touched, abused – violated, even. And for what?! The crab had no idea. Pleasure, it wondered? Fun? Or maybe … Crabs, of course, cannot gasp, but it would have, if it could. Or maybe because I was there. The crab struggled to flip the right way up before something tried to eat it. No, nothing could be that insane.

Some minutes later, and leaving a string of extremely traumatised sea life behind him, Ray McEldroy climbed out of the water. He groaned as he clambered up the slipway to his car and sighed in relief as he released his weight belt onto the tarmac – it was still unpleasantly tight, despite the dieting. After a long and chilly change of clothes, Ray got into his car. It was already getting dark as he set off. It had been a boring dive in bad weather. The only remotely interesting thing had been the crab.

'Strange', he thought, 'it didn't get this dark so quickly yesterday'. In fact, the road looked fairly bright ahead and behind him. 'Must be a storm cloud'. It was weird that it was just above *him*, though. In fact, he must have been in its shadow since before he left, forty … kilometres … back … He stopped and got out of the car very slowly. The road was empty. He looked up and saw a small, totally black disc blotting out the sun. There was some flickering around the edges, but otherwise, for Ray, a *saucer* had replaced the *sun*. 'Crap'. He had just enough time to think before he was hauled up into the air. It was turning out to be one of those days for Ray.

Hanging in the air, without any support whatsoever, Ray looked down and seriously considered having a heart attack. Then he looked up and noticed a circle of utter blackness slide away from the main disc, allowing Thing to descend. He mentally named it 'Thing' because it looked … well … *alien*. It was mostly black, of course, but with red lights on it, about the same size as an LED. It looked sort of like a squid mating unsuccessfully with a bicycle, while trying to fend off an amorous set of fairy lights. The tentacles – as Ray thought them to be – spread out over his body in a not entirely pleasant way. They prodded, probed and *squeezed* in some very tender areas. Then, without any hint of a warning, they let him go. From five metres in the air, back onto the road. It hurt.

# Disconnect

## *Alice Marr*

COLOURS SWIRLED, making different shapes and images. A camera flashed, as a model posed in elegant stance. Zoom. I am the model, transitioning to my next expression, giving the camera a sly grin.

"Wow!" I hear the photographer exclaim, except this word has come from *my* mouth. My eye squints to the eyepiece and I focus on the model, feeling the cool metal from the shutter release under my finger. Flash! The barrel of a gun is pressed between my eyes as I'm being shoved backwards into a dark corner. I stiffen as the finger on the trigger twitches. Bang! Three masked faces dance in front of me, weaving in and out of the eerie woods. The faces contort, as if melting, and slowly drip to the ground, which is fluorescent, and causes me to squint. Click. The brightness disappears, leaving glowing blobs, obscuring my vision.

"Are you able to stand?" I look up. A face stares down at me, brows furrowed, lips in a thin tight line, and a police helmet sitting officially on its head.

Then, suddenly, two hands are hauling me to a standing position. Spin – spin – spin. I'm twirling like a ballerina, never focusing on my blurring surroundings. My feet start moving now, one in front of the other, the steady rhythm like a clock. Tick-tock, tick-tock they go. I can see the whiteness of the police officer's knuckles as he grips my arm, but strangely, cannot feel a thing.

Then, a whirring noise. It gets steadily louder until I can hear nothing but its pounding in my ears. I look around, trying to source the noise. Yet, as I continue moving, it never fades, almost as if it were coming from me. The police officer looks at me, shakes his head and mutters loudly. My sense of my surroundings is strange – some things blurry, some changing colour, some moving closer and others further away. Where I am I cannot tell.

The officer stops suddenly. We are at the entrance to what seems to be a scary and uninviting carnival. A dark figure stands in front of me, leaning forward to reveal a grotesque clown's face. I quiver as he speaks harshly again. Second time this week! This is starting to get out of hand.

"Well, Sergeant, I'll bring it to the office and call Dr. Johnson," the police officer says, then proceeds to pull me through the entrance. I struggle as the clown stares menacingly after me. The carnival is hair-raising, as I pass many different, yet equally terrifying characters. The rides flash and flicker, creaking as they move, bereft of passengers. Instead of music, a metal clanging plays.

As the various elements of this cocktail of happenings register with me, my arm begins to involuntarily rise, then fall, jerkily. The police officer tutt-tutts upon noticing this. He makes a movement that looks as if he is opening a door, except there is no door to be opened.

"In there," he orders, muttering something about calling a doctor.

I try to walk, but my feet begin to sink into the dark grass, making walking a struggle.

"Hurry," he rasps.

I wade to where he's pointing and sit on a chair I hadn't seen till then. My arm is still rising and falling, ears ringing and sight fuzzing and blurring, losing and gaining focus erratically. I sit blindly, uncontrollable jerks pumping through my body for what seems a long time, when two contorted shapes appear in front of me. The dark one, I can gather, is the police officer. The one in white looks almost angelic. This person in white pokes and prods at me, and it seems like I am paralysed because of my inability to pull away from the stranger's touch.

"I am very sorry about this," the man says to the police officer. "Ah yes, its auditory, visual and somatosensory cortices are malfunctioning," he continues.

"Well, you must be more careful," replied the police officer. "We approved this project with the expectations that there would not be strays around the town disturbing the locals."

"I am sorry for it. As you can see, these robots are still not up to scratch. We are working hard in the laboratory, so I must be leaving now. I will turn this one off and have it collected tomorrow, if that is possible."

On hearing these words, I start panicking and the doctor lifts a small silver object to my eyes. A sharp click, then darkness.

# Rivalry

## *Ciarán Morrissey*

JOHN AWAKENS IN DARKNESS. He hasn't the slightest clue as to where he is or how he has come to be here. Is it night or is it day? All he knows is that he is seated with his arms tied together behind the back of a chair and that there is some sort of a rag stuffed into his mouth. A musty smell fills the air and, every time he inhales, he ingests a large amount of dust, causing him to cough very uncomfortably every few seconds.

John feels a searing pain across his forehead. Immediately, images come rushing into his mind in a series of flashbacks. Initially, the flashes are short and hard to decipher, but soon they become much longer and John begins to paint a picture in his mind. He can remember leaving football training. He was the star player and captain of his team, Kilmurry, who were playing in a semi-final this weekend. Everybody in the parish had been talking about it because it was against their greatest rivals, Doonbeg.

As John walks along, he hears the sound of an engine approaching from behind. He turns around and is blinded by the headlights of an oncoming vehicle. He turns away quickly and by the time he has managed to shake off the blinding effect of the lights, a van has pulled up next to him. A man wearing a balaclava jumps out and tries to grab him. John instinctively throws his bag to the ground and tries to fight him off. After an intense struggle, John breaks free and tries to flee. The driver, immediately seeing what is happening, opens the door of the van and John runs headfirst into it. He feels an unbearable pain across his forehead before losing consciousness and collapsing into a ditch.

A sliding door is violently flung open and John is awoken from his musing. Sunlight pours into the van, hurting his eyes.

Daytime! Immediately, John's thoughts turn to his parents. They would be worried sick that he hadn't returned home last night after training. It takes his eyes a while to adjust to the light. All that he can make out is that two men have entered and the door has been slammed shut again.

"Well John, are you comfortable?" asks one of the men, mockingly, as the other bursts into laughter. There is evil in the laugh and John knows that the two men have no good in mind.

"Right, all joking aside, it isn't for the good of your health that we pulled you in off the side of the road," says the same man, pulling the rag out of John's mouth.

John recognises the voice, but somehow can't manage to place it in his mind.

"Who are you, you bollix, and what the hell is all of this about?" roars John, attempting to jump up out of the chair and forgetting for a second that he is actually tied to it.

"Calm down, son," replies the man, putting his hand gently on John's shoulder.

"All we want to do is talk."

"Talk! Are you serious? You kidnapped me just so you could talk? And get your hand off me, you piece of shite, or I'll –"

"Or you'll what, ha? I don't think that you're in any position to be making threats now, are you?" says the kidnapper, mockingly.

"Look, just tell me what you want."

"Okay, okay! I'm sure you are aware of the final on Saturday?"

"Yeah, what about it?" rasps John.

"Well, let's just say that I've got a rather sizeable amount of money riding on this game and, with the playing form that you're in, I just can't take the risk of letting you play. So I'm asking you not to. I don't know, fake an injury or something."

"And what if I don't?"

"Well then, my friend here will give you a real injury." Silence. "So, what's it going to be?" Again, a silence. "Alright so, I'll give you a few minutes to think about it."

And, with that, both men leave the van. John spends the time thinking about how much this game matters to everybody in the parish and how much it matters to himself. After a few minutes the men return.

"Alright so, what's your answer?" No answer from John.

"Come on with it, we haven't got all day."

"I can't do it."

"What do you mean you can't do it?" Yet another silence. "Alright, Jim, do what you got to do."

John can hear footsteps coming towards him, then a pause. Suddenly, Jim lashes out with a right fist to John's jaw, followed by a left deep in under his ribcage. The other man, now standing to the rear, grabs John's hair and pulls his head back.

"What about it now, you little shite, ha? Are you still interested in playing that match?" he asks, taunting him. John doesn't even hear these questions. His focus is on the intensity of pain that he feels in his jaw and stomach. "Alright, Jim. I think he needs a little more convincing."

With that, Jim instantly unleashes another barrage of punches, this time to the chin and the right eye, and, in no time at all, they get the answer that they are looking for.

"Alright, alright," says John.

"Sorry, what was that?" taunts the kidnapper.

"I won't play in the match. Just don't hit me again."

"Alright then, but remember, if you do play, there will be something ten times worse waiting for you." And, with that, both men pick up the chair and throw it out the door, causing it to shatter upon impact. The van quickly pulls away and John lies motionless on the ground for quite a while before he finally comes to his senses.

When he eventually finds the strength to stand up, he realises that he is in a field in the middle of nowhere. He wriggles his arms and legs free from the ropes and looks around, trying to find anything that he can recognise to give him the slightest idea of where he is. He scans the landscape for houses that he might recognise, but there is nothing. He rummages frantically and locates his phone. No bars, but at least he is able to check the time. 9.45am. His eyes widen in shock. His parents will be worried sick about him, he thinks. He quickly hurries to the road and sees a car coming. As it nears him, he realises that it is his neighbour and good friend, Liam O'Connor. Liam recognises John immediately, pulls over and rolls down the window.

"John! What in the name of God happened to you? The Guards found your gear bag on the side of the road. Your parents have been worried sick."

"I was kidnapped."

"Kidnapped!" he gasps, in absolute astonishment.

"Yeah! Look, I've no time to explain it now. Can you give me a lift home?"

"Yeah! Of course. Get in."

When they arrive home, John's parents run to embrace him. When they finally let go of him, John realises that there is a garda in the room as well. He gives a statement, relating everything that has happened.

Over the next few days, John can't get the horrific events of some days earlier out of his mind. He doesn't attend school for the rest of that week. He is haunted by memories of the beating, uncertain of the wisdom of playing in Saturday's final. He knows how much it means to everybody and that he will never be forgiven if he doesn't play.

Saturday. John sits in the dressing room all by himself. He still doesn't know whether he will play or not. Will he do a runner? He looks up at the clock. 2.55pm. Five minutes to go before the match starts. Suddenly, the door flies open and in comes the manager.

"There you are!" he says. "What the hell are you doing in here on your own? Come on, the match is about to start."

John now knows that he will have to play the game. When he emerges from the tunnel, he is greeted by a sea of colour. The green and red of Kilmurry and the black and white of Doonbeg. Suddenly, he forgets about everything that has happened. A surge of adrenaline courses through his veins, as he joins the rest of the team in the huddle.

John goes on to put in a Man of the Match performance, kicking a goal and eight points in the process. And that night, the team members travel back to Quilty, where they are greeted by what seems like the whole parish. The well-wishers are wild with excitement and festivities go long into the night.

Later again, as the crowd disperses, John makes his way to his car. As he closes the boot, after putting in his gear bag, he hears a voice from behind.

"Well, John, remember us?"

# Heartache

## *Alicia von Metzradt*

A KNOCK. That's all it took – a knock. Immediately, Juliette jumps up from her bed. Her eyes widen as they scan for any signs of disturbance. You'd suspect, to look at her, that she'd been told her house was on fire. A single glance at the clock hanging lifelessly on the wall, ticking pitifully, calms her down.

7.37am. Time for school. A disapproving sigh, and she moves across her room to where an array of clothes is laid out. 'Monday,' she thinks. She chooses a plain outfit: a white blouse, a simple pair of jeans and her favourite sweater.

Juliette rummages through her schoolbag, making sure that she has all the correct schoolbooks for the day. She realises there is a pattern to what she wears. Each Monday the same. Tuesday the same as every other Tuesday. And so on. 'Why don't I just label my drawers?' she thinks, then chuckles.

"Morning, Julie," her mother calls, smiling at her from the small round kitchen table. Her hands are wrapped wearily around her first cup of tea of the morning. Mondays never agreed with Juliette's mother. It always took those few cups of tea to get her going.

"Morning, Mum."

A quick look at the kitchen clock. 8.15am. 'A little slow today, Julls,' she thinks, then considers skipping breakfast, just to stay on track. Suddenly, she remembers something.

"Sarah!" she exclaims, but not too loudly.

Her mother glances over the rim of the cup. "Hmm? What was that, Julie?"

"Nothing. It was nothing. Sorry, Mum, I gotta run. Can't have breakfast. Bye!"

And, before her mother even realises it, Juliette has gone. Out the door in a shot, taking full advantage of her mother's Monday morning slowness.

8.34am. The sun creeps slowly over the greyness of the winter clouds. Juliette's friend, Sarah, waits at the corner of a housing estate where she and Juliette had arranged to meet. 8:30am they had agreed. Sarah looks at her watch, then sighs. Juliette is four minutes, twenty-six seconds late at this stage. Sarah hates people being late.

No less than half a minute later, Juliette runs around the corner into a small lane, right into Sarah's view. As she reaches her, Juliette pants, then apologises between gasps. Sarah holds up one hand, silencing her friend.

"No worries, Julie. It's fine, honestly. Now, let's hurry. Don't want to be late." Then, smiling to herself, Sarah walks in the direction of the school, leaving Juliette to catch her up.

A glance at her watch. 12.23pm. Juliette drums her fingertips along the top of the table, making no attempt whatsoever to hide her impatience. Instead of paying attention to her Science teacher, she focuses on the second hand on her watch.

*Tick-tick-tick-tick.* She swore she saw it move back one time, just to agitate her.

*Tick-tick-tick.* And the sound begins to annoy her. She diverts her attention back to her teacher, trying to block out the ticking. But to no avail. Every second word sounds like a tick. Instead of hearing *'Protons, neutrons and electrons'*, she is hearing *'Pro-ticks, tick-trons and elec-ticks'*.

*Tick-tick-tick.* The ticking gets gradually louder. Her eardrums are pulsating with the sound. Then, suddenly, the bell drowns out the ticking. 'Yes!' she thinks. She grabs her books and dashes for the classroom door.

Once outside, she rushes down the corridor, oblivious to the hundreds of others milling round, as they make their way to or from their various classes. She rounds a corner at speed and, suddenly, smacks straight into another student coming towards her. She is knocked to the floor and her books scatter along the ground. She scrambles to her feet, feeling her face reddening.

Just as she reaches for her History book, a hand brushes off hers. She looks up and meets the chocolate brown eyes of Alex Sanders.

"This is yours, I presume?" says Alex.

"Alex! I'm so sorry. I didn't mean to –"

Alex raises a hand and she falls silent, her face now redder than a beetroot. A cross between a smile and a smirk crosses his face as he stoops, picks up her History book and extends it to her.

"It's all right. Accidents happen, after all."

All Juliette can do is nod as she takes her book, not trusting herself to speak. Alex's other hand falls gently to her left shoulder, as he steers her carefully away from the point of collision.

4.20pm. Juliette is ten minutes late at this point. She and Alex had been talking, a budding relationship almost unknowingly developing. She knows she is late, so she tries to enter the house quietly, gently closing the door behind her. Little does she know that her mother is standing, waiting in the hallway. She can be very strict on matters of time.

A heated argument ensues and Juliette stomps up the stairs as her mother shouts after her. She drops her schoolbag by her bedroom door, dashes to her bed and pulls her phone and a piece of paper from her pocket.

Names. Options. Add New Contact. *A-L-E-X* she types, then saves. And then, the message: *'Sorry, Alex, can't go out on Saturday. Grounded.'* Send.

She drops her phone onto the bed, retrieves her schoolbag from the other side of the room and begins her homework.

*Beep-beep-beep! Beep-beep-beep!* 7.30am. Juliette hits the power button on the clock, as she throws back the sheets and hops out of bed. Suddenly, the flashing of her phone catches her attention. A text. Alex. Dated yesterday at 6.07pm. Damn! She missed his reply. She wonders if he is mad, but one look at the text reassures her. '*Hey, no problem. I'll see you in school and we can meet up after your grounding has ended. x*'

Phew, it was all right. And he has signed off with '*x*'. '*How sweet!*' she thinks, as she replaces her phone and gets out her typical 'Tuesday' clothes. She chuckles lightly as she remembers her little joke to herself from the previous day.

She runs down the stairs, ecstatic. Her mother is sitting at the kitchen table just as yesterday, but is a little more awake this morning.

"Julie."

"Good morning, Mother," Juliette replies, trying her best to smile, to be agreeable, polite.

"I've decided that, provided you're home on time for the next two days, your grounding will be lifted."

Juliette is surprised. She throws her arms around her mother's neck and hugs her tightly.

"That's great! Thanks."

Juliette dances across the kitchen to where the bowls are kept. She hums softly as she makes her breakfast. Then she hears the phone above in her room and makes straight for it.

*Beep-beep*! Vibration. Flashing. Another text. Alex. She opens eagerly. '*Meet me at the front door at 8:50. I have to talk to you.*'

Juliette stops when she reaches the entrance to the school and checks her watch. 8.47am. She is early – that is good. She leans her back against the wall, bends her leg and rests the flat of her foot against the brickwork.

Some minutes later, Alex turns the corner. His eyes brighten when he sees Juliette waiting.

"Hey, Julie!"

"Oh, hey there, Alex! You wanted to talk to me?"

"Yeah, I did. Come on and walk with me," he says, gesturing with his hand, and he walks ahead of her.

As she follows, she feels confused. She tries to figure why she is feeling nervous. She stays silent. Alex mumbles a few words and glances occasionally over his shoulder to see if Juliette is still there. She tries to initiate a conversation, but all she gets is a garbled mumble in response.

Suddenly, Alex stops. So too does Juliette, a few paces behind. He closes his eyes as he sighs. A long ten seconds pass as Alex appears to mull over some thought or other.

"Juliette …"

"Yes, Alex?" Juliette replies a little too quickly, too eagerly, perhaps.

"Juliette, I like you. I really like you. For ages I've liked you. And … from what I've heard, you like me too. So, I was wondering if, y'know, you and me …" Alex gestures with his hand, making small rotations, trying to get his point across without actually saying it.

It finally clicks with Juliette. Alex is asking her out. He wants her to be his girlfriend. Why, then, is she just standing there? Why doesn't she say something? She's just making a complete fool of herself, right in front of him. She shakes herself, pulls herself together.

"Yes, Alex."

Alex then suddenly pulls her against him, hugging her gently, his chin resting on her head.

"Thank you," he murmurs against her hair, then kisses her forehead. Juliette pulls away and looks him in the eyes. "Any day."

Juliette heads for the day's classes. Even those she detests most – French, Irish and Business – can't dampen her good mood. All she can think of the whole day long is how Alex asked her out. How she and Alex are now 'together'.

School over, out the gates and Juliette rushes after Sarah.

"Sarah! Hey, Sarah, wait up!"

She catches up with her friend, breathing heavily, but still buzzing over what had happened earlier in the morning.

"Hey, Julls!"

"Sarah, guess what?"

Sarah glances at Juliette. One look at her face and she knows. Juliette has been talking non-stop about Alex since she bumped into him. So it was pretty obvious.

"Ale–"

"Alex has asked me to be his girlfriend!" she interrupts. "Me, Sarah!"

"Oh, that's brilliant, Julie! Brilliant!" Sarah smiles at her. She is truly happy for her friend. They natter as they walk. Sarah, Julie, Alex and school matters is pretty much the most of it.

When they part company, Juliette runs home and straight up to her room. She texts Alex immediately, still ecstatic over what has happened. 4.04pm. On time. One more day, then she can meet up with Alex. One more day.

*Beep-beep! Beep-beep!* Every time Juliette hears her message tone, her stomach does flips and fills with butterflies. Always Alex. And always she replies immediately. The only time she leaves her room and sees her family is at dinner. Then back immediately again.

Over time, Juliette begins to get more and more attached to Alex. She is seeing her family and friends less and less. All the ties with everyone who'll be there for her, no matter what, are slowly being broken.

Alex knows that if he wants anything, all he has to do is say it to Juliette and she'll hop to it – happy to do whatever he wants. Juliette is completely oblivious to the reality that Alex is slowly wrapping her around his little finger.

A text. Juliette opens immediately. Unexpectedly, it's Sarah: *'Hey, Julie, you able to come out later? x'*

Juliette bites her lip as she replies: *'Hold on a moment. I'll check it with Alex, see if he has anything planned.'*

Then, a response: *'You know what, forget it! Your life revolves around him now. So go, go and run off with Alex, like you want to!'*

No further contact.

Tuesday, 23rd February, 11.06am. A few weeks have passed since Alex asked Juliette to be his girlfriend. Juliette is waiting outside her first class after break when she sees him pass. Instantaneously, her heartbeat quickens and she feels blood rushing to her cheeks. He looks over at her and she waves, grinning widely, but he just ignores her and walks on. She is stunned, dejected, suddenly confused.

For the next few classes, Juliette's mind is in a state of turmoil. 'I'll text him later', she thinks, before she turns her attention to her class once more. She tries getting through it by not thinking of Alex. This works well for a time, until his face slowly creeps back into her mind. She glances at the clock. 3.58pm. 4pm, and the bell rings. Juliette is out of her seat like a hare.

Once home, Juliette, as always, makes for her room and grabs her phone. *'Hey. Why were you ignoring me earlier? x'* she texts. His reply comes instantly: *'Meet me at the front door at 8:50. I have to talk to you.'* The identical text he sent almost two months previously, before he asked her out. She lies back against the pillow, grabs her book and opens it.

Juliette sits up in her room all evening, thinking. Reading hasn't helped. She ponders what he'll have to say. She considers texting Sarah, then just deletes the message halfway through it. Time and turmoil take their toll and, gradually, she drifts off to sleep.

8.49am. Juliette waits where she should be, at the front entrance. Early, just like the last time. Suddenly, Alex walks up behind her. She hasn't heard him coming.

"Juliette," he begins, obviously desperate to get whatever it is he has to say over with. He has used her full name: not a good sign.

"Yes, Alex?"

"I … I'm sorry, Juliette. It's over," he says regretfully, then turns his back to her and walks off.

An emptiness sweeps through her. She steps inside the entrance. She hasn't expected this. The person she cared for most leaving her just like that, with no explanation. She drops her bag to the ground and looks at the notice board in front of her. 'How Do You Feel?' is emblazoned on one of the pinned-up posters. She stoops, rummages in her bag and then pulls out a thick, black permanent marker. She looks again. 'How Do You Feel?' She pops the lid off and writes in big, bold, black letters: **NEVER TRUST BOYS**. And she feels the tears spill out onto her cheeks and trickle down her neck.

# Scouted

## Keelan Cunningham

THE SWISH OF THE NET, the roar of the crowd and that adrenaline rush that courses through your body. It is a sequence of events known all too well to Gareth O'Connor. Gareth jogged back into position, the smile of satisfaction of scoring yet another goal for Templeogue Celtic spread broadly across his face. He glanced over towards the sideline to where his manager, Dara O'Brien, was standing with another man. Gareth figured the stranger to be in his mid-forties, with greying hair and a welcoming face. The man was talking to Gareth's manager, smiling and nodding his head. The young footballer turned away again, his smile stretching even further across his face.

When the final whistle blew, the score was 2-1 in favour of the Templeogue Under-16s, both goals courtesy of Gareth O'Connor.

"Gareth!" Dara shouted. "Come over here for a sec."

Gareth jogged over to where Dara was standing, the other man still at the manager's side, his eyes fixed on Gareth. It had been a long time since Dara himself had taken to the field, his pot-belly showing the effect that years without physical exercise had taken on him.

"My friend John here wants to talk to you. He's on the coaching staff with Rovers."

Gareth turned towards the other man.

"Well done, lad. You played a blinder," John began. "I'm very confident the club would be extremely interested in you."

Gareth was buzzing with excitement, but he tried not to let it show.

"I'm going to get a scout to come and see you play."

"Thank you very much. That would be brilliant!" said Gareth.

"Nice to meet you, Gareth. Good luck!"

"You too!"

The man walked away, seemingly satisfied with his discovery. The board at Shamrock Rovers would be happy with this, he thought to himself.

Gareth's mind was haywire as he made his way home through the streets of Dublin. He might actually get a place in Shamrock Rovers youth set-up and all he had to do was impress some scout. Sure, the League of Ireland was a long way from the Premiership, but he had to start somewhere. He was dazzled by the possibilities of what could come of this. Things were finally starting to get better for him and his mother. Nothing much had gone right for them since his Dad died a few years back. Money was hard to make and his mother had had to get a part-time job down at the supermarket, just to make ends meet. So, Gareth had to take care of himself most of the time.

He walked in the kitchen door to find his mother getting dinner ready. She smiled warmly at him as he entered.

"So, did ye win?" she asked.

"Yeah, 2-1."

"How did you play?"

"Scored a couple, should've got another."

"And did that man come to see you?"

Gareth pretended to be puzzled. "What man?"

"Come on, you know exactly what I'm talking about! What did he say?"

"Oh, not much. He's just getting a scout to come see me play!"

"Oh, Gareth, that's fantastic! I'm so proud of you."

Gareth's mother jumped up and down with excitement, almost knocking over the saucepan in the process. He hadn't seen his mother this happy in years.

"And even if you're not accepted, you're still the best to me!" his mother added.

"OK, Mam, thanks." She smiled at him and hugged him tightly. "Now, what's for dinner? I'm starving!"

Saturday. In the dressing-room, Gareth wasn't joining in with the usual pre-match banter. He was focused on one thing and one thing only: impressing that scout. He was handed his usual No. 8 shirt, central midfield. He traced the number on the back of his shirt and pondered what might be.

Once out on the pitch and into the warm-up, he didn't dare take too many shots for fear a few bad ones would put the scout off, if he saw them. What was he thinking *if* he saw them? Of course he would see them. He would always have his eyes fixed on Gareth. In fact, Gareth could feel them now, staring at him, burning the back of his neck.

The match kicked off. Gareth started slowly, feeling his way into the game, trying to look as impressive off the ball as he was on it. But he needed to be more eye-catching, which was hard, considering the opposition. They were playing St. Pat's Youths, the toast of Dublin. No one stood out, but as a unit they were very impressive. Gareth was trying everything he could, but aside from a few good flicks, tricks and tackles, he couldn't break the Pat's defence down, not by himself anyway.

It was nearing the end of the game and Gareth still felt he hadn't done enough to impress the scout. He looked over at him now. He was constantly jotting things down on his clipboard and his face remained steely, fixed into a cold hard stare. Gareth tried to forget he was there. One chance, just one chance was all he wanted. The game was almost over when he finally got it. He sidestepped one of the opposition in midfield and could immediately see his route to goal. He rounded another player on the edge of the box and saw the goalkeeper begin to rush out towards him. He drew back his leg to shoot. He wasn't going to miss, he couldn't miss. Just as he was about to strike the ball, their big lumbering centre-back took him out with a flying tackle from behind. It was an obvious penalty and Gareth wasn't going to let anyone other than himself take it.

He got up and dusted himself off. The fact that the defender had been sent off barely registered with him. He placed the ball carefully on the spot and took three slow steps back. He had already decided where he was going to put it. He eyed the keeper and the keeper eyed him back. Then Gareth lowered his eyes, started his run up and struck the ball with all the power and venom that he could muster.

Gareth sighed as the final whistle was blown. He turned to walk off the field when he heard Dara's call:

"Gareth, come over here for a sec!"

# Night-time

## *Amanda Honan*

AS I FELT THE WATER *course up and down my nostrils, my face grew ever paler. My skin wrinkled rapidly from lack of oxygen and I was drifting in and out of consciousness. Fighting hard against the swallowing of water, I began to tire, and then my awareness began to wane ...*

"Get up, Martina," my mother shouted.

"I'm coming," I called out, sleepily.

My body froze and a shiver ran down my spine, as she pounded up the stairs. With every step she took, the thudding noise grew ever-louder. I hopped out of bed and pulled my working clothes out of the wardrobe. I had to wear a pair of black shorts and a red apron that was now a kind of dark brown colour because it was covered in congealed blood. As I pulled up my shorts, I glanced over to the small white clock on the cupboard. 3.30am. The rays of light from the moon were peering through the bottom of the blind. This was the usual time she came in from the pub.

My mother, Helen, reached the top of the stairs. For a split second, we stared into each other's eyes, then I quickly glanced away. Then Helen stumbled and staggered in the direction of my little green room. I backed myself into the corner of the room and closed my eyes tightly. I tried to imagine I was in bed asleep, but it did not work. I could hear her banging into the door and then the cupboard, knocking something off it. I was too scared to even open my eyes to see what it was.

And then the noises stopped. I waited a minute, then opened my left eye slightly to see where she was gone. She was standing there with her hand outstretched, just waiting for me to move.

My whole body started to shake. I began to imagine I was in my now-dead father's arms, resting my head on his chest, while he told me the story of the three little pigs. How long ago was that? Four, five years? Yes, five. He had died in a motorbike accident when I was only four years old.

Suddenly, reality hit home again. I felt her hand on the scruff of my neck. She dragged me to the ground, hitting my head against the wall on the way down. I landed with a thump. She lifted her left leg and kicked me in the ribs with her red stiletto. Pain coursed through my body.

"Shut up screaming," she howled, kicking me even harder – this time in the head. I felt a warm liquid fill my mouth. I swirled my tongue around within. Blood! One of my front teeth was gone. Then, grabbing me, she pulled me up by my hair. I saw her clench her fist, then BANG! A punch straight into the face. Blood splashed from my nose, splattering onto the green wall beside me. Then she staggered and stumbled her way back out of the room, bumping into the wall and then the door.

The tears streamed down my face, as I climbed up onto my single bed and curled into a ball. Pain surged through my body, owning me from head to toe. The blood gushed in what seemed like torrents, drenching the pillows with its redness. Then it abated to a constant trickle, which meandered its way from mouth to chin to bedclothes. My tooth! What was I going to tell my friends at school tomorrow?

My mother, Helen, always has her hair scraped tightly back into a ponytail, not one strand out of place. She wears a perfume that has a lovely scent of freshness – that same freshness you get when you go down to the beach and deeply inhale the fresh sea air. This is Helen before she goes to the pub. But when she comes in from the pub, her hair is messy and the stench of alcohol and cigarettes would make you sick. It's only at these times, when she is drunk, that she turns her violence on me. It had been such a normal happy family before my father died …

"Martina, get in here now, you stupid little girl." The unexpected bellow jolted me to reality. I swivelled on the bed, stood out onto the floor and painfully made my way to her room. The only remaining picture of my father had been swept from cupboard to floor – shattered. Tiny pieces of a life, now gone. The tears mounted, then fell hard and bitter and plentiful. As my crying abated and I gathered myself a little, I realised that there was no longer anybody else in the room. I turned, and there, in the corner of this huge yellow room, was a load of empty wine bottles. A noise distracted me and, as I turned a second time, I realised that she had crawled inside onto the *en suite* bathroom floor and was lying there laughing to herself.

I walked in. The cold tap was running into an almost full bath. Suddenly, she sprang up and caught me fiercely by the hand. I could feel the bone in my wrist momentarily pop out of place. The pain! The agony! She grabbed my leg with her other hand, catching me unaware, and flipped me into the ice-cold water. The sound of one deadly thump of head against enamel was dulled by the density of the water. I floated to the top. The bloated red apron was the only thing keeping me afloat. I felt her hand press against my chest, and then she pushed me under!

As I felt the water course up and down my nostrils …

# Gravity

## *Calem Roelofs*

ME. MY CAR. A BEATEN ROAD in a so-called 'City of Hope'. The sight of homeless people lining the walls and pavements as far as the eye can see ignites a spark – a thought – in the recesses of my mind. Not so many years ago, these people would have been housed, fed, clothed and just living in acceptable conditions.

It is a world that now is collapsing upon itself – these mere melted American dream droplets now adding to the tide of recession. Disgraced into having to sleep on bare asphalt, these unfortunates end up using cardboard and newspapers to warm their limbs.

Though regarded as little more than wild animals or stray house pets, society's concern for them is marginal at best, and not one middle-class, suit-wearing person would even raise his head to notice. Yet this is only because these middle-class, suit-wearing folk are constantly afraid that they might end up like these homeless, disregarded by the modern age.

The big-shot rich snobs look down on these people as if they are mere dirt on their shoes, a smudge on their ideal utopia, only to be wiped off and thrown into a waste bin. Do you think they would even notice the people who could be scavenging through their bins for a mere morsel of food? Most humankind would worry about silly things like looks or love affairs, while these hordes have to worry whether or not they will survive the night.

As I drive along, the cries of people begging for loose change flood my ears. I contemplate it all. Then, unexpectedly, I get a call from work. My boss waffles on for a while about how the company has been hit hard by the recession and how shareholders are pulling out. Somehow, I know what's coming. I brace myself

… and then: "Bill, thanks for being a great help over the years, but we're going to have to let you go. We're sorry."

I gulp, knowing that I am swallowing the last of my pride.

# Penalty

## *Maria Murphy*

A BEAD OF SWEAT ran down the side of Maura Flynn's face. She glanced at the football, neatly positioned at her feet. She could still hear the crowd chanting, although the separate cheers of 'Ballykilne!' and 'St. John's!' had merged to become more of a single, muffled drone. Maura raised her head and found herself locked in a stare with familiar eyes, and she couldn't muster up the strength to break it. She was, after all, tired out from the football match, now nearing its end, and the outcome of which would be decided by her next move. As she held her stare, Maura's mind drifted back to another time ...

Since she and her family had moved to Ballykilne three months ago, Maura had settled into her new school well. She had made friends quickly, and had got to know even more of the girls in her class since joining the school football team. Already, Maura had been one of the best players on the team at her old school and now, after just a few training sessions, she had earned herself a spot on the starting panel of the Ballykilne Community School side. They had a very strong team and since Maura had joined the panel, they hadn't lost a single match.

The trouble had started when Ms. McSweeney had called the team in for a meeting on Monday. The girls were all still on a high after winning their quarter-final the previous week. Their coach, and favourite teacher, had announced that they would be playing the semi-final on Tuesday of the following week.

"Don't get too confident now, girls. A place in the semi-final does not guarantee a place in the final!"

But it was what she said next that really caused Maura distress: "We'll be playing St. John's Secondary School from Kildrum and they won't give us an easy win!"

St. John's! Maura's old school. The school where all of her oldest friends went – the school for which they all played football. What could she do? Throw the game and give up a chance to play in the final? Betray her old team? Several uninviting options filed hauntingly through Maura's mind. She thought about telling Ms. McSweeney that she had injured her ankle and wouldn't be able to play. But even the thought of lying like that made Maura feel guilty – she couldn't just abandon her new team right after they had made her feel so welcome at the school. But neither could she betray her old team – she still felt a part of it.

"Oh, yes, and our captain on the day will be Maura Flynn," announced Ms. McSweeney. Maura was stunned. This was really going to complicate matters for her.

"Maura, Maura!"

Maura blinked out of her daze, suddenly realising that Tara Lynch had been talking to her. Tara was a friendly girl, who had been one of the earliest to talk to Maura on her first day and had since become one of her closest friends at Ballykilne.

"Maura, are you okay? You haven't said a word since Ms. McSweeney told us you were going to be our captain for Tuesday. You're not nervous, are you?"

Maura made to answer but, before she got a chance to reply –

"Because it's not really a big deal. I was captain for a match a few weeks ago, remember? And it doesn't involve any hard work or anything ... So, there's no reason to be worried!"

"Mmm ..." mumbled Maura, deciding on the spot not to tell Tara what was really bothering her.

"Oh, wait, I think I know what this is really about."

"You do?" responded Maura, nervously, and her face reddened.

"Yep!" said Tara. "You're worried that if we lose, Ms. McSweeney and the other girls will blame you!" A triumphant smile lit up Tara's face. "But don't worry, that won't happen. There's no way we're going to lose to St. John's. We played them in a challenge match at the start of the year and we beat them no problem! And that was before we had you!"

"I know," Maura replied. "I was captain of the losing team."

"What? No way! St. John's is your old school? Wow!" For once, Tara was stunned into a silence. After what seemed like a very long time to Maura, Tara found her voice again.

"But, why didn't you say anyth–? Wait, is that why you were so quiet all afternoon? Duh! Of course it is! Maura, this must be really hard for you! I'm sure Ms. McSweeney would let you sit the match out if you explained it to her, though! I mean, she can't really expect you to play against all your old team mates, can she?"

"Yes she can, and she will, because I'll be playing *with* all my *new* team-mates. We're not saying anything to her." Maura was sure of this. It was her problem, not her teacher's, and she wasn't going to change that. Tara looked confused.

"But what are you going to do?" Good question, thought Maura, as she walked away.

"Okay, girls, do a cool-down lap, then stretch out and you can go home," instructed Ms. McSweeney. "But remember, we're leaving at 9 o'clock on Tuesday. So, be in school early!" And so ended their final training session before the semi-final.

As they walked back to the changing rooms, Tara asked Maura if she knew what she was going to do yet.

"I'm just going to go out there and play my best, and if my old friends are angry with me, then it's their problem, not mine!" announced Maura.

Tara was surprised at how quickly Maura had come to a decision. As certain as Maura was at that moment that this was the right thing to do, a phone call that evening changed her mind again. The call was from her best friend since playschool, Aileen Waters, who told Maura that she would be captaining the St. John's team.

"So, are you going to be playing on Tuesday?" asked Aileen, anxiously.

"Well, I can't really back out now," said Maura, hesitantly, "I'm supposed to be captain."

"Oh! Well, I guess I'll see you then. Bye, Maura," said Aileen, curtly, and then was gone. And Maura could feel the accusation behind the words, knowing that Aileen and the rest of her team would consider this a complete betrayal, and leaving Maura with a worry-filled weekend.

Tuesday, and Maura still found herself in the throes of indecision as she awaited tip-off. She was playing in mid-field and, thankfully, as she was marking a girl in the year behind her, she didn't know her that well. Maura's brain was working overtime as she pondered all the possibilities. She could let the younger girl win the ball from the throw-in and then, afterwards, make an honest attempt to try and win back possession – that would be fair to both teams, wouldn't it? But she didn't think she would ever be able to look Ms. McSweeney in the eye again if they were to lose because of a score she gave away.

The referee blew the whistle and suddenly the game had started. Ballykilne had possession and, not long later, Tara, who was playing full-forward, had put the ball in the back of the net. Maura's heart leaped with joy upon seeing this and she felt like this was her team now. So, she should spare no effort in supporting them. However, when St. John's scored an equalising goal at the opposite end of the pitch and Maura felt herself filled with the same sense of pride, she really was confused.

The match went by in a blur. Maura vaguely remembered winning some balls, but she also remembered losing some. She was trying her hardest, but the younger girl was really putting it up to her. St. John's and Ballykilne were tied in scores. Any point that one team managed to score was matched at the other end of the pitch, and time was nearly up. Maura was just thinking how much she didn't want to have to play a rematch when the referee blew his whistle. Maura looked up to see someone in a blue Ballykilne jersey lying on the ground, obviously injured.

"Tara!" cried Maura, sprinting towards that end of the pitch. One of the St. John's backs had fouled Tara inside the square and the referee was awarding a penalty. As she was helping Tara up, Maura heard Ms. McSweeney call:

"Maura, I want you to take the penalty."

"What?" was all that Maura could say, and she came towards the teacher.

"Please, Maura, I know this match has been hard on you, but it's the last kick of the game and you're our best free-taker. Just take the shot and, if you miss, it's okay." Then she paused a moment. "Though, obviously, we'd all prefer if you didn't!" she added, clearly trying to lighten the mood. Maura couldn't think of any way to refuse, so she mumbled something to her teacher and walked over to where the referee was waiting with the ball in place. Maura took three steps backwards from the ball and looked up. Instead of the usual goalie, Aileen had stepped into the goals to try and stop the penalty.

Maura's dread had finally caught up with reality. In a matter of seconds, all the happenings, all the turmoil, all the expectations of the past few days coursed through her thinking. But seconds felt much more like a lifetime. Refocusing on what she had to do, she tensed herself for the shot. She smiled weakly at her old friend, then watched as Aileen readied herself for the kick. A blink, a steadying of hands, a deep breath. Then an anticipatory sharp intake of breath from the now captivated crowd as Maura's foot struck the ball.

# Forever in Time

## James O'Connor

"THE BOAR! Go get him, son. This kill is yours!"

Leo's adrenaline was pumping as he charged through the dense undergrowth. Already, he had a full view of the animal. Briars and nettles scratched the boy's legs, but this was of little consequence to him. Food this grand was worth a high level of pain.

Suddenly, the trees parted and both boar and man found themselves in a clearing. Leo stopped, drew his trusty bow and arrow and pulled back on the string. The arrow soared through the air and hit its target with deadly accuracy. The boar ran on for several moments, then keeled over to one side. Dead.

In no time al all, Leo's father and brother were on the scene. They tied the legs together and heaved the beast onto their shoulders. It was the eve of the Winter Solstice – that time of great importance for the Celts – and already, the evening sun was dipping in the sky. A great fire was to be lit in the Crannóg as soon as darkness descended, and more folk would assemble and take part in various rituals. A great opportunity for Leo – as he was now coming of age – to make new contacts.

Leo and his fellow-hunters entered the huge, round, wooden enclosure through the main fence. Festivities got underway as soon as the sun had set and the longest night of the year began. The bonfire was lit by Leo's father, an ageing man who showed obvious pride in hosting the event.

Almost as soon as the fire engulfed the pile of wood, screams of terror erupted from around the Crannóg. Leo sensed danger and his blood ran cold. Before he knew it, two men seized his arms from behind and tried to knock him to the ground. But Leo was strong and broke their hold with relative ease. Glancing around him, he could see young men and women being subdued by these peculiar-looking attackers. These people were not wearing the animal skins to which Leo was accustomed. Rather, they were clad in silver fabrics and had black skins wrapped tightly around their feet. A surge of rage filled Leo's every sinew, dismissing all confusion. The youth was known to have an extremely bad temper. He clenched his fists and readied himself for war.

Grabbing one of the men who was holding a young woman hostage, Leo wrapped his arm around the assailant's neck and jerked it to the right, snapping the spine instantly.

"Hide! Hide! In the huts, now!" he ordered, as he ran with the young woman in search of his weapon. He grabbed his bow and arrow, then turned to face the chaos. His only view of the insurgents was occasioned by the eerie orange glow of the fire, which danced on the attackers' faces. Many of the innocents of the tribe stood in his way and he could not take steady aim at the marauders. Then, suddenly, Leo had the breath knocked out of him as he was tackled to the floor. He hit the ground hard and was immediately weighed down by the body of an attacker. Another man, wielding a knife, ran over and knelt down beside him. A searing jab pierced Leo's arm and he roared out his pain. Despite his struggle, the numbers were too much and he knew he could not fight them off. Another jab into his arm and Leo saw the light dance in his eyes, then fade to black.

It was not the familiar sound of a crowing rooster that awoke Leo the next morning. Rather, it was the clank of metal and the slamming of a door that made him bolt upright. It took several moments for him to gather his memory of all that had happened and, in that time, he tried to comprehend his new surroundings. He was sitting now on a flat iron bed in a cramped and stuffy boxroom. Something like a prison cell, without any basic amenities.

As the memories flooded back to him, so too did his fury. Though he had never seen any place of habitation of this sort, instinct dictated that he take out his anger on the door. He pounded hard against the wooden division, hollering as loudly as he could. The banging and shouting reverberated far beyond his cell and, before very long, he heard the rushing of feet moving towards the room in which he was imprisoned. The door opened and a man and a woman stood in the opening, each wearing silver garments of the type that the attackers had worn the night before.

"My name is Dr. Paul Newman, and this is Dr. Christina Newman. Please follow us and all will be explained," said the man, in something of a casual tone. Sensing the man's apprehension, Leo moved cautiously as he followed them out of the room.

They led him through a corridor, which was as dull as the cell from which they had come. Then into another cell, containing a steel desk and three small chairs.

"Take a seat, Leo," ordered Christina, who was clearly much more sure of herself and not aggressive in her speech.

"Leo," began Paul, "you were born here in this very building and, as a baby, you were transported thousands of years back to the past. Now, as you have had time to grow strong, we have brought you back to your own time period, where you belong." He stopped briefly to allow Leo to digest this much.

So many questions were circling in the youth's mind that it was almost overwhelming. "Wh ... wh ... why have you done this to me?" he asked.

"You see, Leo," Christina answered, "you were born into a dangerous world where disease was rampant. We sent you to a much healthier time in Earth's history, where you could grow strong. Now it is time for you to be brought back to the present, so you, along with other young people of your generation, can repopulate Earth and secure humanity's future."

None of this made sense to Leo. Something was clear, however: he had been taken from his true home, his people attacked, and these people were responsible.

"Take me home, now," demanded Leo.

"I'm afraid we cannot do that. Your family members fully understand the situation and are willing to comply."

Leo's rage was building. He was starting to despair.

"Let's go and meet some of your people, shall we?" suggested Paul, seeing Leo's mounting desperation.

As they stood to leave the room, Leo decided he had to act now or never. He grabbed a chair and stared at Paul with a look of insane anger. Then, he swung the chair with all his strength, striking Paul's head with one of the legs. His body fell on the table and slid onto the floor. Not knowing if he was dead or alive, and not caring either, Christina made a mad dash for the door. But Leo was too quick for her and grabbed her, covering her mouth with his hand.

"Take me back now, or I'll snap your neck like a twig!"

She nodded, conceding defeat, and Leo released her. Tight-lipped and eyes focusing on the ground, she led him through the corridor and into another small room, which this time contained a large grey machine with sliding doors. Christina stepped inside.

"Well, get in!" she said, in a patronising tone. Leo was wary, but knew nothing of this world to make a proper judgement. He stepped in and the doors shut tightly behind him. Christina pressed some symbols on a keyboard and, in a blinding flash of light, they had travelled through time.

As the doors opened, Leo noticed how the temperature had dropped considerably and the previously grey surroundings were now replaced by the luscious green environment to which Leo was accustomed. Christina knew she was no longer in her own world, but was, rather, now in an ancient, natural setting of which she had no knowledge. No sooner had they stepped out of the machine than it seemed to suddenly disappear from view. They had arrived directly outside the main gates of the Crannóg. Leo banged on the doors, but no one came to open.

"You see, Leo," Christina screamed, "your family has forsaken you. We are all you have now."

Suddenly, in as strange a way as it had disappeared, the time machine returned. Immediately, four men dashed out to assist Christina. Slowly, they edged towards Leo, who now backed himself up against the fence. All seemed lost, and Leo's spirits began to sink into despair. Unexpectedly, and with bewildering speed, the mighty gates swung open and there stood Leo's brother and father, standing with bows and arrows at the ready.

"Aim, FIRE!" they roared, as they unleashed their missiles. Arrows sailed through the air. Two of the four men were killed instantly. Leo caught the bow thrown to him by his father and aimed a primed arrow directly at Christina. Their eyes locked on one another and he could see that her previously hard demeanour was now reduced to true and genuine fear. The tension was building in the string and he could barely hold the arrow. Just then, out of the corner of his eye, he spotted a far better target. The arrow was released with deadly accuracy. It hit the large button on the time machine, destroying it completely and trapping Christina in this great age forever.

# Intuition

## *Alanagh Hunt*

'*HER NAME IS RIO and she dances on the sand, just like that river twisting through a dusty land, and when she shines, she really shows you all she can, oh Rio, Rio, dance across the Rio Grande*'.

I paused, silently taking a breath as my MP3 player continued to shuffle through my library of music. I've always had a tendency to sing aloud and tonight was no different, as I made my journey home from Joanne's house. The walk through the meandering paths of Oak Grove, about one kilometre from where I live in Bellbridge Heights, would be totally unbearable if it wasn't for my mechanical pal to occupy me. I felt that night had fallen quickly since I departed for Joanne's after dinner. A sharp breeze rose and I could feel every follicle of hair stiffen on my neck.

Occasionally, I quickened my step in the hope of hastening my arrival to my living-room fire. I began searching the various music genres on my device, my fingers suffering every touch. Suddenly, the thought hit me! 'Why not take the short cut through Bellbridge Cemetery?' It takes at least ten minutes off the journey and, given the weather, this route seemed the better option.

As I entered the resting place, I blessed myself. The street lights illuminated each headstone. I walked along the perimeter of the area quite swiftly. I regularly used this route on my journeys home – usually during the day, however. A breeze rose and the branches of the oak trees clattered together, creating a frenzy of falling leaves. My breath weakened and an eeriness descended, causing my heart to race and my eyes to widen at what I saw before me. 'Monica Kelly. 1990-2006. Died age 16. November 2006'. My name! My age! Momentarily, the number '6' seemed to rotate and become a '9'. I rubbed my eyes in utter dismay and looked more closely. Yes, 2009. But then, almost as quickly again, it reverted to 2006.

I stumbled, feeling the stingy sensation on my wrist as I backed into a bouquet of nettles. What stung me even more, though, was the date. 'The date? The date?' My emotions were in turmoil as I tried to comprehend the incomprehensible. Today was the 18th of November 2009. I began questioning myself. Groping in the dark, I regained my bearings. My lungs were clouded and breathing had grown strangely painful. Deep breaths – in-out, in-out. My stomach began to churn and I felt incredibly wheezy. Thankfully, it stopped, but only after I had vomited all over poor Charlie O'Hara. I had one last look at the headstone and then bolted home.

Silently, I slipped into the house, managing not to disturb my family, who were watching their Thursday night soaps on television. Heading straight upstairs, I showered immediately. I showered for a long time, as though believing that would cleanse my mind of what had happened. No sooner out of the shower when a physical exhaustion hit. But my mind wouldn't allow me sleep. It raced and turned, replaying every step of what had happened earlier. I could feel my heart pumping, pumping, pumping in rhythm with my breathing. I stared unthinkingly at the wall for what seemed like hours. My digital clock read 3.20am. My sighing broke the silence.

*"Pardon the interruption, but could all students participating in the walkathon this lunchtime please report to the reception area at 12.30. Thank you."*

School work was the last thing on my mind and so was the stupid walkathon. I resolved not to utter a word of any of the previous night's events to anyone. How could I begin to explain the situation? My family, my friends – all would think that I was losing my sanity. Perhaps my decision was wrong, but I'd rather die alone.

My surroundings seemed more dangerous to me, now that my deadline neared. I was accepting fate. There was no other option. *My* name was marked on that dreaded headstone. What I questioned most was why and how. Why me? How would it happen? My destiny seemed to hang over me like a cloud – a very heavy cloud.

"Monica! Monica Kelly! Are you paying attention to me?"

"Oh, sorry, Mr. Kennedy, I … I … I tuned out for a second. I'm really sorry!"

"OK, young madam, but you better keep up or there'll be consequences. Now start on the chapter on cell division."

My close friends began whispering about my unusual behaviour just before we set off for the walkathon. I felt so devious keeping what I knew from them. The girls were so happy, but next day their high spirits would fall because of my death. I dreaded the thought of putting them through the trauma. We walked throughout the town in groups of five or six, Vice Principal Ms. O'Brien leading the way. Fortunately, the weather was dry and the ground was covered with crispy, dead leaves from the wicked night before. I walked and erased all of the negative thoughts I had and joined in fully in the conversation with the girls. They, as girls do, gossiped about Michelle and Aidan, who were apparently dating in secrecy. As the chatting and personal questions continued, we noticed that we had fallen behind all of the other groups. They were many yards ahead of us and Ms. O'Brien, besides being partially blind, didn't notice our straying. The six of us found humour in our lack of concentration and briskly jogged in hope that she wouldn't notice our absence. The five of them sped ahead of me, as I paused momentarily to catch my wheezy breath. Before I knew it, they had run to Relish Avenue to join the others. I changed into sprint mode. I felt tiny beads of sweat trickle down my nose into my open, panting mouth. When I reached the end of the footpath, I stumbled upon a loosened brick. I fell over it, thundering onto the road, feeling the burning sensation of the impact of concrete on skin. My vision was impaired with tears. I gathered my shirt to dry them. Suddenly, a truck turned a blind corner and approached with speed in my direction. An overwhelming sense of anxiety crept up on me. I was gripped by a crippling weakness and defencelessness. Closer and closer it came and then BEEEEEEEP!

My clock-radio deafened me, as I woke in a cold sweat. My pyjamas clung to my skin, my hair glued to the back of my neck. The relief of wakening, of finding myself alive! I had no idea what brought on such a terrible nightmare. I reached out for my phone and momentarily held it away from me, allowing my eyes to adjust to the details on the screen. A calendar notice appeared on screen: 'November 20th, 2009. No event'. I was completely puzzled as to why it appeared on my phone. I didn't set any reminder for today. I did not dwell on it any longer and headed downstairs for breakfast.

"Good morning, Monica! Did you sleep well?".

"Yeah, Mom, thanks." I grabbed myself a bowl and started pouring my cereal, noticing that some spewed out across the table.

"Monica, love, could you turn on the telly for me, please?" I switched it on and Mom began channel-hopping. She flicked onto RTÉ 1. Breaking news:

*"Reports are coming in of a schoolgirl being killed in a hit-and-run accident in the town of Bellbridge, Co. Wicklow, late yesterday afternoon. Gardaí have asked of anyone with knowledge of the incident to make contact with them at Bellbridge Garda Station, 053-9125565. That number again for Bellbridge Garda Station is 053-9125565."*

# Collapse

## *Killian Geaney*

TO NIALL'S RELIEF, the bell rang and he was finished. Another day down. Walking towards his bus, he was aware of somebody walking behind him, getting closer and closer. Unexpectedly, a hand caught hold of the back of his jumper and started pulling him towards the oil shed, where nobody could see him. As Niall put up a fight, he got a knee into the back, which knocked him for six.

"Hey, Fatso, give me your money," one of the large boys said. "Did you not hear me?"

Niall couldn't concentrate on what was being said to him. All that concerned him was the excruciating pain in his lower left side. His kidney, he guessed. Another painful blow hit Niall, but this time it was a wallop into the stomach.

"Answer me, Tubby?"

"I don't have any money," Niall pleaded.

"Well, you better have some tomorrow or you're a dead man, do you hear?"

"Yes, yes," said Niall, and they let go of the tight grip they had on his jumper. He ran around the corner, still in pain, but trying not to draw too much attention to himself.

Still dazed, Niall made his way onto the bus and slouched in his seat. Even the paper balls being fired at him could not distract him from what had just happened. He could feel his heart racing in his chest. Once at his stop, he staggered his way off the bus and walked slowly towards the house. He stopped, fixed himself up a bit, stood up straight and went inside.

Slowly, he made his way up the stairs, trying to step precisely on each step, so that the creaking noise wouldn't be as noticeable as usual. He was used to going to and coming from school without any interaction with his mother, because it was usual for her to be away at this time of the day.

Since his father died, Niall and his mother had struggled to pay the bills and keep the house. It had resulted in his mother working two cleaning jobs, which kept her away from home all day. It had put a serious strain on the family and Niall didn't want to add to her load by further burdening her with this problem. He tried to creep his way upstairs, so his mother wouldn't hear him. But no such luck.

"Ah, Niall, I didn't hear you come in. How was your day, love?"

"Ah, grand, sure. Actually, we got loads of homework, so I might go and make a start on it."

"Alright, love, I'll give you a call when dinner's ready."

The mention of food brought all of the other thoughts flooding back to his mind, the words 'Fatso' and 'Tubby' spinning around in his head. Yes, that must be the reason that this is happening to me, because I'm fat, he thinks. Well, I'll change that. "I don't think I'll bother, Mam. I had a big lunch."

"Alright, that's grand."

And Niall went upstairs and closed his bedroom door behind him, crumpling onto his bed. All his energy was gone. Sweat poured down his back in torrents and an appalling pain gripped his innards. But, despite the pain, he fell asleep quite quickly, drained of energy, listless.

It was 7.30 when the alarm bell rang the next morning. Niall couldn't believe he had slept that long. Still in his uniform, he found himself covered by a reasonably flimsy blanket which, he presumed, his mother had thrown over him. Niall hopped out of bed in his usual fashion, but a severe pain again coursed its way across his stomach. He whimpered gently, lifted up his shirt and was shocked at what he saw. A row of purple and blue bruises contoured together, forming a mesh-like pattern. He touched the vulgar-looking skin ever so slightly, but even this sent a rocketing ache raging through his body. Despite his effort to present as normal, the whole episode of the day before was still flashing through his mind. Not mindful of the fact that the only reason that he was being bullied was that he presented an easy target, he decided that the only way of resolving the situation was for him to lose weight. Now, he was determined to do it, and there would be no need to mention his dilemma to anyone.

The pattern continued over a two-week period. Once a week he would be set upon and would have to give any money he had to Seán Scully and the other boys. He had come to learn their names by listening in on the usual banter between the other lads in his year. It seemed that Seán and his mates had been involved in numerous incidents in the school, one resulting in suspension for what was rumoured to be a smoking-related matter. These attacks would happen at any time during the day, making Niall paranoid from the first bell in the morning to the last in the evening, and still believing that it was all because of his weight. Niall had resolved to lose weight very seriously and had barely eaten anything in the past two weeks.

Niall came home that evening with more bruises on his legs and stomach. The thumpings were growing in intensity. At this stage, he was beginning to question why they were still happening, still in denial that it wasn't his weight that was the problem. He had become increasingly obsessed with monitoring his weight and was frustrated that he was getting no results.

The next day passed and, to Niall's relief, he had managed to get through unscathed. Listening into the conversation at break with the lads, the rumour was mooted that one of the girls in the Leaving Cert class was anorexic. For the many in the group who had never even heard of anorexia, one of the lads was quick to enlighten them. Niall was riveted as he listened to his comrade speak.

He went home that evening, frustrated yet again at seeing no signs of his weight receding. Having eaten dinner, he went upstairs to do his homework. He couldn't get the thought of the girl who was anorexic out of his head. He went into the bathroom and locked the door behind him. Lifting up the toilet seat and holding back his jumper, he leaned over the bowl. He attempted to stick both his index and middle fingers back in his throat, but retracted them immediately when he got the feeling of nausea. But he persisted until, finally, he vomited.

Over time, as the beatings continued, so too did the vomiting. Niall would religiously make his way to the bathroom and throw up. The whole routine had become something akin to an addiction for him. It didn't help, either, that now he had shown visible signs of losing weight. Neighbours who visited the house would compliment him on his trimness. But this only threw fuel on the fire. It simply encouraged him to vomit more and more.

In time, signs of something not being right began to register with Niall's mother. She had noticed that he was losing weight rapidly, that he was looking an increasingly deathly pale and, despite sleeping 14 hours a night, that he seemed to be constantly tired. But when she commented on this, Niall just shrugged and dismissed her remarks as being of no import.

January 24th. Nothing could have prepared Niall for what was going to happen. He started the day feeling a bit more tired than normal and with a slight pain in his chest, but just brushed it off as being related to the beating he had got two days earlier. Lunchtime had passed and the pain had intensified, but he was adamant that he would see the day out. As soon as the last bell rang, everybody rushed for the school doors. Making his way along the congested corridor, Niall was mindful of his light-headedness and of an increased intensity in the pain. That's when it hit: it was as though his chest had been suddenly locked into a vice and squeezed. And then, collapse.

Niall's mother stood helplessly by his hospital bed as the pulse of the life support machine faded to a nothing …

# Predator

## Sophie Cassidy

*MELODY IS ALERTED by the coldness of the water lapping at her ankles. The events that have led her here file like marching soldiers through her mind ...*

Monday, 12.25pm. A group of 5th Year girls point at a blond-haired boy at the other side of the hall. Their high-pitched giggling irks Melody. This time it is notably squeakier than usual and she is eager to get away from it.

"Oh, my gosh! He's so cute!"

"Did you hear what David said?"

"He likes that Melody girl ..."

"Is he nuts?"

"Melody? Isn't she the girl who has just gone by?"

"Weirdo!"

"Loner!"

Melody quickly ducks into the changing rooms behind them. It's nothing she hasn't heard before. Girls like that have a tendency to be highly unoriginal.

Eventually, the giggling fades and she is left alone, searching for her phone. It has to be here somewhere, she thinks, as she looks about the place. In her frustration, she picks up a stray towel and flings it across the room. Suddenly, she hears the faint sound of wind chimes under her gym bag. What the heck is that? Then, the bag follows the towel. And there, ringing on the bench, is a small silver phone. It's definitely not hers – far too expensive. It is signalling a message on the screen. Her curiosity gets the better of her and she opens.

12.36pm: MY MELODY! YOU DON'T KNOW ME YET BUT I KNOW YOU. SEE YOU SOON.

It takes her a minute to realise the message is for her. A chill creeps down her spine. What's with this phone? she wonders. And the message? And how could this person know her? Her stomach heaves a little as the words sink in: *My Melody!* She stuffs the phone into her bag and heads out the door.

She feels as though everyone's eyes are following her as she shimmies into her navy raincoat. Don't be ridiculous, she tells herself. Why in the world would anyone pay attention to her? She hugs her arms, keeps her head low and walks out onto the footpath, taking care not to look back at the school.

Lunchtime is spent mulling over the mysterious message. Theories are mounting in her head: a cruel prank, perhaps? She knows she isn't the most popular girl in school, but there isn't anyone with a particular grudge against her, either. And the wording is so bizarre – *My Melody* … Is it just a prank? Or is it something else?

She has just discarded that theory when, just after Biology, as she leaves the class, the wind chimes sound again. Her stomach heaves.

2.41pm: THERE'S SOMETHING FOR YOU IN 285.

285! Her locker number. It should scare her that this person seems to know so much about her, but instead she feels really excited. The months she's spent in Ballykin have been dreadfully monotonous and, strangely, this stands out as the first bit of excitement she's experienced in ages.

She can't focus in Maths and can tell that Mrs. O'Donnell is getting fairly cheesed off at her apparent lack of interest in numerators. She's ill at ease and jittery, irksomely tapping her fingers on the desk in front of her. O'Donnell gives her a cold, chastising stare. Melody is dying to get to her locker to see what is inside.

Class over. She walks determinedly towards her locker, ignoring the stares of her fellow-students. It takes only seconds to dial in the combination and, sure enough, dangling from the coat hanger at the very back, is a locket.

Excitement is replaced by terror. It isn't the fact that her name is engraved across the gold plating. It isn't that he knows which locker is hers or even that he knows the combination. It is the photo within the locket. Clear and close-up. The background is almost black, but she can easily make out the surroundings. It had been taken at night, while she was asleep in her bed.

She feels nauseous and dizzy. The ground seems very far away. How did he get this? Who is this? She stops herself short, fighting hard to dismiss the thought that is mounting in her mind: Stalker.

Goosebumps rise and work their way up and down her spine. She shoves the locket into her bag and grabs her jacket. There must be some mistake, she thinks. There's no way this can happen to her. She's a recluse, a loner, a nobody. What interest can anyone have in the likes of her? Indeed, more than interest, it would seem. The raindrops pound against her umbrella as she moves hastily down the street. It is a relief to step into the warmth and safety of home.

"Mom! Mom! Are you home?" Her voice is shaky. She needs to know she isn't alone.

"In here, honey!" Relief.

"I'll be upstairs doing some homework, okay?"

"That's grand. Dinner will be ready in about an hour."

She takes the stairs two-at-a-time, into her room and straight to her desk. The computer is old and takes its time kicking in. She scans the faces of her classmates in a photo taken three months ago. She feels sure that this person is in the school. Who can it be? Who can it be?

"Mels, dinner's ready!" calls Mom. Enough for now, she thinks. She can look again in a while.

Later, when she returns to her room, she hasn't got the mental energy to study the photos more closely. Bed seems a better option. But her mind will not switch off. In the darkness now, she flicks incessantly from message to message, combing every possibility in her mind. Her eyes soon grow heavy with the effort and she feels herself begin to drift towards sleep, when suddenly:

11.23pm: YOU CAN'T HIDE, MY DEAR. I CAN SEE YOU.

The blood drains from her face as she reads those words. She senses danger. He can see her, she thinks. She glances at the window. The curtains are still undrawn. She climbs out of bed, her feet shaking until they are steadied by the cold floorboards. Imaginings that, at any minute, a hand might grab her from under the bed are coursing through her mind. She rushes to the window and fumbles with the tassels. The curtains fall closed and she jumps back under her duvet and, in time, drifts into a deep and troubled sleep.

The morning sun peeps through a gap in the curtains. She sits up, her eyes adjusting to the light. The room is cold. Then the creeping, dulling tone of wind chimes.

Tuesday, 8.13am: WATCHED YOU CLOSE YOUR CURTAINS LAST NIGHT. YOU CAN'T KEEP ME OUT, MY LOVE, SO DON'T TRY.

There are black rings resembling bruises under her eyes. She pulls on the previous day's clothes and shovels down some cereal before rushing off to school.

The day passes in a whirl and he doesn't text again. She's relieved, but she knows he isn't gone. He's still watching her. She knows it. All day long a presence lurks at the back of her mind. It never goes away. She's sure that she's being followed. She doesn't know what he wants, but she can't help thinking his intentions are malicious, sinister, dark.

When she arrives home at the end of the day, she is terrified to find Mom's car gone. There's a note in the kitchen.

"No!" she whispers under her breath. She locks the doors and windows and closes all the curtains. Curled up on the sitting-room floor, she can hear every squeak. She is sure that she hears footsteps coming towards her. No matter how hard she tries, she can't block out the nightmares. What does he want from her? Whatever it is, he's sure to get it. It seems inevitable.

4.37pm: I KNOW YOU'RE ALONE. I'M COMING.

And now hysteria takes hold and she begins to sob uncontrollably. Logic should tell her there's no way he can get into the house. Instinct presages that she's in danger. The Garda station, she thinks, but then the thought of ringing them just seems too embarrassing. They'd think she's insane. Suddenly, there's a loud banging on the front door. Her heart jumps. Her pulse is racing and she is trying very hard to catch her breath. It is as if the whole room is spinning. Then it goes fuzzy, as she fades out of consciousness.

She knows nothing of her Mom finding her on the floor, and that it is some hours after that that she wakes up in her bed. It's dark outside. Her immediate instinct is to check the phone: no new messages. She gets up and heads downstairs.

Mom is watching *News at Nine*.

"You're awake! Are you alright, dear?" Mom sounds concerned. "Should I call the doctor?"

The last thing Melody wants to do is worry her.

"No, it's okay," says Melody. "I didn't sleep too well last night, that's all. It must have been that cup of tea before going to bed."

"Alright. Well, try to get some shut-eye tonight."

She raids the fridge, reluctant to return to the loneliness of her room.

12.30am. Into bed. The curtains are already closed, so that's one worry off her mind. Teeth grinding with the effort, she tries to direct her attention to anything other than the image of her stalker. Her eyes begin to droop and minutes later she's asleep.

Another restless night. She wakes up several times, positive he is in the room. At one point, she turns on the lamp and searches every nook and cranny before dozing off again.

Next morning, she leaves for school early and gets there in time to do the homework she had forgotten about. She's on guard all day. It is as if he is hiding in every shadow, waiting for her. A predator waiting for the right time to strike. Hunting her.

The day passes by in a blur. She can't focus on anything. Everything seems so surreal, almost as if she's having an out-of-body experience.

Wednesday, 3.21pm: YOU CAN'T ESCAPE. I'LL SEE YOU TONIGHT. BELIEVE ME.

And she does believe him. Not that she knows what she'll do about it, but she's certain he will come. It is at this point that she begins to wish she'd never been born. Walking around in a trance at home, there's nothing to do but wait. Wait for the inevitable.

She does all she can to secure the house. She locks the windows and doors, sets the security alarms and even places a large butcher's knife beside her bed. There'll be no sleep tonight.

12.43am: I SEE YOU. I CAN'T WAIT.

The curtains are closed. How can he possibly see her? She is riveted by fear. She hears a light, methodical tapping on her window. She can imagine the cruel, obsessive eyes peeping hungrily through the glass. There is nothing she can do. She sits, silently waiting for the tapping to stop. Maybe, if she doesn't move, he'll think she's not there. She steels herself, musters up the courage and looks out through the curtains. Nobody's there. Just a patch of condensation on the window pane, where he had been breathing.

She quickly closes the curtains again and crawls back to bed. Her head is hot and pounding. Just like the pounding on the door the previous day. She tries to ease her muscles, but it's no use. The claustrophobia enshrouds her, as she stares out into the darkness.

3.30am. She wakes with a start, her back damp with sweat. The pyjamas stick to her skin. She turns on the lamp. Every thought is focused on the impending doom and the vivid nightmares. She reaches shakily for the phone.

3.32am: TIME TO FACE THE MUSIC.

Is he here? The sound of wind chimes once again fills the silence, but this time it doesn't come from the phone.

Both the windows and the curtains are wide open, and there, hanging from the curtain pole, is a set of chimes, ringing eerily in the night breeze. "He's here!" she says aloud. The words barely escape her lips before the utter hatred floods through her veins, and she snaps.

"Wh-e-r-e a-r-e y-o-uuu?" she roars. But no reply. Nothing but her heavy panting as she grabs the knife and menacingly slices the air. She slams the window, ties the curtains and collapses to the ground, sobbing. The tears pour down her face as she realises the naked truth: Mom's car is nowhere to be seen outside. Then a renewed burst of adrenaline begins to course wildly through her veins. It's time to end all of this. She knows what she must do.

The sky has already begun to brighten slightly. Her heart pounds as the stairs creek beneath her weight. She shudders to think who might be listening for her down there. Outside, the air is crisp and the street is barely visible. The courage that had seemed so resolute begins to recede as she steps out onto the beach. Exposed. A victim begging for her enemy. She walks slowly, cautiously to the water's edge. She holds the phone aloft. Vague rays of moonlight flicker across its silver casing, as she flings it from her.

3.41am. The stalking footsteps, just twenty feet behind her, fall soundlessly on the sand. Closer, closer, closer. And now the coldness of the water laps even harder around her ankles. With fists clenched and teeth chattering, she wades even further into the icy water …

# Eccentricity

## Jaden Creagh

THE KLAXON ROARED in Ambassador Klag's star-hopper, orbiting the mid-civilised planet Earth, as he had poured his latte into the force-power core instead of the disposal chute. As the small ship descended, he looked over his objective to find a suitable additional race to Pi Empire. Already, the wolf-like Lupins joined his stereotypically alien race (The Mexiods) in the Empire, and these Humans would be, though bland in physical prowess, a good addition.

It took a while for Klag to realise that he was pondering in the face of a canine being. Quickly, he set up communication by speaking common English, in human dialect, but to no avail. Then he remembered Humans were primates of hairless features, and not as boring as this. He registered the dilapidated, slum-like urban metropolis, then he registered true sentient beings, walking along paths beside a large track where primitive, petrol-powered vehicles whizzed past. The Humans were very basic humanoid beings, with blandly stylised hair that seemed to be used as a crest. Curious, he listened to their dialogue. He fell back, appalled. Discourteous, crude, dishonourable and quite a few other 'dis-es' on their manner and intentions.

Klag set off for one of the ghetto-like apartment blocks to further survey these foul-mouthed creatures. The main disadvantage of humanity is overpopulation of one planet. He might, in the long run, be their hero. He leaped, grappled onto the window ledge and examined it: glass. He laughed. "Oh-oh! Wait, it's double-glazed!" he muttered, sarcastically. Basically, walking through, he examined and scanned the unstylish symmetry. A Human sneaked – well, more blundered than sneaked – in and stared at Klag. It disturbed him that the Human seemed to grimace and then, for some retarded reason, screamed. So Klag, irritated, clambered out of the window and up the other one. Again, it was the same deal. He began to wonder if this was an 'idiot tower'.

The klaxon roared in Mexiod Ambassador Klag's star-hopper, orbiting the mid-civilised planet Earth, as he had poured his latte into the force-power core instead of the disposable chute, with severe consequences. His chair rocketed from its hinges and slammed him heavily against the cockpit window. A rain of syringes from the biology unit lashed down at Klag and three pierced his violet, amphibian skin. He looked at one – its contents a dextral compound. Then, another of the same. He'd probably get a headache from muscarine. He looked at yet another and then went turquoise. It was the 'random' bionic syringe, created by a Lupin, one of the Pi Empire's races. Lupins were wolven brutes who were either warriors or psychotic biologists. He calmed himself, saying it would only cause some temporary growth or some such. It took a while for him to realise that his ship had descended upon a cubical, concrete tower, beside which many squabbling, hairless primates walked. Then Klag found that there were thousands of these inadequate crowded towers. None of the primitives could see past Klag's ship's cloaking device, so he began his descent.

Klag began to feel queer as he descended the building, windowsill by windowsill. Suddenly, one windowsill gave way. Klag toppled, but did not attempt to stop himself, for he was too appalled to find his hands and feet had changed into claws.

The crowd was only slightly befuddled as Klag fell with a thud, thinking him to be some sort of deranged, decorated actor. He frantically raced through the mass, growing a millimetre with each bound. As he ran frantically, his mind buzzed. No matter what he tried to tell himself, he knew he was turning into a Lupin. He crouched upon a flimsy, primitive vehicle and looked up at the ironically full moon. Only one moon for this planet. A strange giddiness overtook him and he giggled maniacally. Then sense came back to him. He took out his LRC long-range communication device and dialled the number of the fleet Triagula, the closest Starfleet he knew of. An armoured Mexiod appeared on-screen. Klag spluttered out his whole crisis story.

"We are, unthankfully, having trouble entering systems past Alpha Centauri, because the Gamma Empire is setting up a raid around that area," the captain said, with a slight hint of fear in his voice.

"How long until you break through?" Klag asked, in a deadly whisper.

"About four to six hours."

"Well, it's only about five hours until I'm changed beyond healing."

The captain was slightly taken aback. "Good luck, Ambassador," he said, then closed communications.

Klag was now in an extremely bad state of mind, twitching madly. His now animalistic mind surged out furious ideas. He was going to blast this overpopulated planet to smithereens. *Overpopulated*: the word hatched a brilliant idea. This race would be a perfect ally. Oh, but of course, his *other* mind would have its say.

He neared the cottage in the field in a manic fashion and grappled onto the window. Already, the Lupin Fang Escort Ship was looming above. As he entered, he encountered a 50 year-old man doing some gastronomic exercise. The appealing rusticity of the atmosphere made Klag placid enough to say hello. The humanoid turned around, amazed. At that, Klag's com-pad buzzed on and he was greeted by a wolven face.

"Ambassador, is it an alliance meeting or a resource raid we are on?"

Klag felt the Human's reaction would choose the answer.

# Silent Grace

## *Lanci Marshall Borota*

GRACE'S HEART IS FILLED with loneliness as she sits on her bed. It's the first day of the Christmas holidays. She should be happier than this. A glance to the end table on her left and she sees the picture of her boyfriend, Dylan. And to her right, a picture of her Dad. The thought of her father being in another country saddens her.

"Grace?"

"Yes?"

"How was your last day of school?"

"Fine, as always, Mom." She turns towards her Mom and tries to crack a smile.

"Is something bothering you?"

"Nope. Just bored, I guess."

Her Mom motions towards the window. "You should take Bella for a ride out. It hasn't frosted today. Sure, it's cold, but the fresh air would do your mind some good." The pause is awkward as Grace just stares out the window. "You can give your father a call if that would help. You've been thinking about him, haven't you?"

"I'll call him later." Grace grabs her MP3 player and makes for the bedroom door. "See you."

"Cheer up, honey."

"Yeah. Thanks, Mom. Bye."

Down the stairs and out the door. Her Mom watches and, even from the inside of the house, she can make out the faint pulsing noise of the music to which Grace constantly listens. She glances out the window and sees her daughter gently tacking up her horse.

As Grace mounts the animal and sets off down the lane at a trot, the music fills the air. Thoughts of where to go are constantly filing through her mind. The bay? The town path? Indecision.

"Thank you for listening to Spin Southwest on this winter day! We hope you have a great start to your holidays! We're kicking it off with ten Spin love hits in a row. So, bundle up and enjoy."

Dylan! I'll go to his place, she thinks to herself. The love hits from Spin seem to influence her decision. She ruffles through her pockets while her horse picks at leaves on a sloping tree. She takes her mobile from her pocket, removes an earphone and dials.

"Hey, Dylan. Can I come to yours?"

"I'll be home in about 20 minutes. Take your time."

"Where are you?"

"Only feedin' the calves. So I'll see you soon then, yeah?"

"Yeah. Bye, Dylan."

No answer back. She assumes he's just busy.

Grace gathers the reins, pockets her mobile while replacing her earphone, and urges Bella on. The path is bumpy and quite stiff from the cold. Bella stumbles once or twice as she makes her way through the barren grass. The winter chill has caused the animal to seem quite uptight and strong. Grace knows that concentration is needed and yet her thoughts still wander.

Dad, Dylan, school flick through her mind. Joy, sadness, frustration – not necessarily in that order. Her Dad is back in the States. He would have gladly made the move if he didn't have a few new medical practices recently opened. He has always admired her courage and cool head in odd situations, even though she's quite awkward. Their bond is constant, despite their being two years apart.

Her mobile rings its quirky tone and, suddenly, Bella bucks and takes off at speed. The horse's wind-blown mane and strands of Grace's flowing hair mingle in a vortex, and suddenly, the sense of movement beneath the rider is violent and uncomfortable. She reaches for the reins but clumsily grabs at thin air. A dissonant cacophony of music, ring-tone and cold air bombard her senses. A hectic blur. One boot, then the other slips from its stirrup and Bella's flank rams hard against a wall, trapping Grace's leg. Screams. One final buck and she is thrown to the ground.

Grace lies on the flat of her back and looks skywards. One earphone dangles. The other still pumps its haunting beat into her mind. No feeling. She struggles to move, but all that comes of it is a feeble grunt from deep within her throat. Immobilised. Her eyes function. They dart from side to side, taking stock of her environment. Mobility is gone, but emotion seems still intact. Already, the possibilities of what may or may not be course through her mind, and she begins to cry.

Horse gone, feeling gone and she is in the middle of nowhere. What chance that she'd be stumbled upon? Zilch, she figures. At least she has her music to ease the wait, however long it may be.

Ugh, Newsflash! Just when I really need music, the news comes on, she thinks to herself. Her air of calm surprises her.

*'This is an urgent broadcast for those in the immediate and surrounding area of Tubber. Gardaí wish to alert the public to the escape of a male patient from the psychiatric unit of the Mid-Western Regional Hospital in the past two hours. The man is approximately five foot nine in height, brown-haired, and, is reported to be wearing a white hospital gown. He is known to be dangerous and to have killed previously, and Gardaí caution the public against approaching him. The escapee is reported to have an extreme breathing problem, which induces wheezing. Members of the public are advised to remain indoors until he has been apprehended. Any sightings of the man or any information regarding his whereabouts should be reported immediately to the Gardaí. We'll keep you updated here on Spin Southwest.'*

Dylan cannot contain his anger. She has blown him off. She is never more than 20 minutes late. But he has her mother's number and, for once, it comes in handy.

"Hello, Mrs. Dawson?"

"Yes?"

"It's Dylan."

She'd always known he was a bit of a hot-head, but also that he loved Grace very much. This time his anger is very apparent to her.

"Is something wrong, Dylan?"

"Any idea where your daughter is? She seems to have forgotten that she was coming to my house."

"She left here about an hour ago. I haven't heard from her since ... but ..."

Mrs. Dawson thinks back to the shocking announcement she'd heard on the radio. "Dylan, do you think she's OK?"

"Yeah. Why wouldn't she be?"

"You didn't hear the emergency broadcast?"

"Emergency broadcast? No."

"Dylan, there's a killer around the area."

"A what?"

"Oh, my God! Dylan, we need to do something. We need –"

And suddenly, the line goes dead. No sooner cut off than Grace's mother has dialled 999.

"Emergency services. Which service do you require?"

"I haven't heard from her ... my daughter. She's out on her horse and she probably hasn't heard about the killer. I haven't heard from her ..." Her throat tightens as she speaks. "I'm afraid she may come into harm's way."

"Please give us your details. We will assist you in every way we can."

She slumps down by the window and the wait begins.

Meanwhile, Grace is helpless. She could never have imagined how unbearably horrifying it would be to panic on the inside, yet remain physically still. Her heart is racing at the thought of the maniac being at large. She wonders how long she has been planted there. At least three hours, she figures.

Suddenly, her ears pick up on something. She listens closely to the music pulsing. Quite an irregular beat. It's as if a dog is barking on the bass line or a call is echoing her name in the lyrics. Her heartbeat fills her ears, drowning it all out. Pulsing. Throbbing. She can hear herself breathe. Wheezing. Wheezing? She remembers the remark in the broadcast. A wheezing psychopath. Her eyes swivel from side to side. The noises get louder by the second.

"Grace! Grace?!" It's a cry from the north, clearly one of desperation.

'Dylan', she thinks. 'I know it's him. God, he sounds so close'. Her heart pounds even stronger. She thinks she hears him call out yet again. The sounds of howling dogs and whirring sirens mingle in the distance. Footsteps. Wheezing. A low cackle, coming nearer all the time. Thoughts echo. Sweat rises. Her mind spins, thinking of who will reach her first, fearing who it may or may not be. The Gardaí. The escaped patient. Her father. Her father! She didn't even get to make that call to him. Her heart thumps louder than the music now. The calls and noises seem to be drawing closer, all coming to one centre. She knows she could be leading Dylan to his death, but what takes rank above all else is that she never made that call.

# Shoot Out

## *Conor Murray*

'YOU HAVE 48 HOURS to give us the money, or trust us, you'll regret it', the anonymous letter reads. Tyler has been getting death threats for some time now. The one prior to this had said that his head would be chopped off and hung on his headstone …

Tyler is a kind man, but, unfortunately for him, he mixes with the wrong people – the sort with whom most people don't want to get involved. But Tyler needs the money.

Some days ago, he was distributing 'goods' to reliable customers when he was spotted by the Gardaí. Fortunately for him, he just managed to get away through some alleyways and shortcuts on his everlasting Honda 50. Stricken with fear since that incident, he had not communicated with The Blue Eagles, and so, had not been able to give them the €8,000 owed. Tyler retired to sleep that night in fear of the days that lay ahead. However, days and nights passed by without any hint of a death threat, or worse.

Wakening on Friday the 13th, he notices the town is unusually quiet and ominous black clouds dismiss any prospect of sunshine. Fearing attack, Tyler hasn't left his apartment for many days past, but he is quickly running out of food. He hasn't eaten in days. Half a sliced pan is all that remains and that, by now, is well past its sell-by date. He ponders what he wouldn't do for a Domino's pizza right now, then quickly dials their number.

"We're sorry, but your balance is too low to make this call. Please top –" *Smash!* Before the poor lady could finish her recorded message, the phone is unceremoniously smashed in *smidiríní beaga* and scattered around the already untidy floor.

"Damn!" yells Tyler. He has no choice now but to go out in public and try not to be seen by either the Gardaí or his gang.

3.22pm. Front door. Tyler is ready to go. A hoody and two jackets cover up the cushion that gives comfort to his stomach. A peak cap holds his concealed dreadlocks in place. His freshly beardless face gives him a totally new appearance. Not a bad disguise, he thinks.

After some moments of intense and silent prayer, he finally plucks up the courage to leave the comfort of his home. The rusty hinges squeak noisily as he opens the rickety door. It is in bad need of a few slaps of paint, but right now, that is the last thing on Tyler's mind.

A good one hundred metres walk to the nearest grocery store lies ahead of him. A series of relief-filled sighs accompanies his every stride. He passes the Old Folks' Home, where usually the teenagers look for some attention, but there is nobody to be seen. Then, on his left, comes the church: amazingly, not a soul to be seen there either. Wind gusts whirlingly around the town and a looming sense that something is going to happen permeates the air. Tyler has an eerie feeling that he is being secretively watched. He has no idea who the watcher may be, but he can most certainly sense that he is under someone's furtive gaze.

Forty metres from the shop now. All is quiet – quieter than it should be. Thirty metres. A lengthening of stride and the clipped and frequent sound of his leather-soled shoes against the pavement increases. Twenty. His hands start shaking with fear now. Almost there.

The last ten metres, then *Bang! Whissssp!* He could feel the bullet brush past his head. *Bang!* Another one, this time just inches off his head, smashing the shop window behind him. Where are they coming from, he wonders. What can he do? No time to think now. *Bang!* A perfect shot. And Tyler falls to the ground, holding his injured left shoulder. His mind is spinning. He is in total shock, yet somehow, he has expected this.

Tyler can hear the faint sound of a siren amid the chaos. Strangely enough, he welcomes the sound. Within seconds, a drama ten times better than any on Irish television is unfolding around him. Brandon, the leader of the gang, has his pistol in line with Tyler's face.

"Where the hell is the money, Tyler? You should have known better than to betray us. We expected it a week ago, but we never got it, did we? Trust me, Tyler, you're going to regret that. I'm sorry, my old friend, but you've left me with no other –"

"Drop the gun and hands above your head," the inrushing garda roars. The sturdy guardian of the peace has his gun pointed at Brandon. But, showing no sign of obeying the guard's orders, Brandon holds his gun firmly pressed between Tyler's eyes. Tyler's shoulder is piercing with pain, but there is only one thing concentrating his mind right now. One question: who will be the first to shoot? *Bang!*

# Get Away

## Laura Mulqueen

"Don't you " – SLAP! – "ever" – PUNCH – "speak to me like that again" – KICK.

I felt the gush of warm blood fill my mouth. I coughed it out before it choked me. Knelt on all fours, I threw up a mixture of blood and vomit. Then, heaving again and again, I collapsed on the stone floor, exhausted. My chest was thumping, my eyes blurred from the tears. The smell of alcohol burned like acid in my nose. After catching my breath, I crawled to the bathroom and, fighting my aching muscles, I hoisted myself up on the counter.

I was lucky, considering the circumstances. A couple of loose teeth, a swollen lip, a cracked rib, maybe. I had to admit I had had worse. I changed my clothes and began the laundry. Unfortunately, it was a chore that kept only my hands busy. My mind was whirling. The train ticket in my jeans pocket seemed to weigh a hundred pounds, as I busied myself around the house.

Later that night, while listening to my father's snores from across the hall, I crept quietly to my dressing table and searched for the sock in which I kept my Credit Union savings. Then I rehearsed the procedure in my head again. There were only two people to whom I could go about this. Sleep proved uneasy that night. I tossed and turned and dreamt the worst.

Six o'clock the next morning I found myself silently sneaking out the front door. Pulling up my hood, I concealed my battered face and set off swiftly towards the city. I glanced back nervously from time to time, terrified of being caught and dragged home again. My heart was pumping so fast that I thought it would burst from my chest. I felt the blood vessels in my face dilate as I approached the entrance to the train station. Detouring to the ladies' toilets, I locked myself in a cubicle. Then, extracting a scissors that I had borrowed from the art room two days previously, I closed my eyes tightly and began to cut my hair, wincing slightly as I heard it slither softly into the toilet bowl. Flushing it away, I turned towards the mirror and stared in at my new-look spiky hair. Then, though in the grips of horror, I made myself move towards the exit.

9.30am. My composure was no better, as I sat nerve-racked on a Limerick-bound train. My Dad would notice my absence about now. I half expected a burly Garda to come charging up the aisle, bellowing 'Robyn Brown'. I tried to calm myself, focusing instead on the song blaring from someone's headphones. Despite my trying to remain inconspicuous, I attracted horrified stares from seemingly concerned passengers. Turning my face away, I stared dejectedly out the window.

Two trains, four hours, 11 towns, 269 people later, I stepped into Heuston Station, Dublin. No time for dawdling. I headed straight out onto the street and crossed over to the Luas stop. Mere seconds later, the tram slowed to a smooth halt within inches of me. I hopped on and grabbed a railing hastily, as we shot off again on a curving, snake-like journey of the city and its southern suburbs, ultimately coming to its terminus in Tallaght. I stumbled off – my head reeling – and wandered around a while. Then, spotting a taxi that was free, I hopped in and handed the address to the driver. I texted the registration number of the taxi to my aunt and settled into the seat.

The driver looked like he was pitying me. Being mindful of the condition of my face, I knew what he was thinking. He struck up a conversation.

"So, what parts are you coming from?" It may have been that he was trying to be friendly, but I wasn't taking any chances.

"Clare," I responded.

"And what brings you to Dublin City?"

"Just visiting my aunt and uncle," I replied, with an innocent smile.

He took this as an encouraging sign and prattled on about the weather. I nodded now and again, not really in tune with what he was saying.

The stopping of the taxi brought my reverie to a halt. The driver grinned back at me. I handed him some notes and thanked him, then climbed out of the cab. I had barely had a chance to interpret my surroundings when a shriek of horror caused me to spin around.

"Robyn! Your face! Come here to me, pet," said an overly dramatic Aunt Emmer. My face wasn't that bad when I checked this morning.

"Your hair," she moaned. "Your mother's beautiful hair! What have you done to yourself, child?"

I winced as she hugged me. I followed her into the house, as she muttered to herself.

"Bit lanky!" she said. "Spuds will fix that. And pale! Sure, a bit of work out in the sun on the stalls will bring some colour to your cheeks."

Her thinking aloud brought a smile to my face – the first time I had smiled in months. She led me into her kitchen. It was square and cosy. Sunshine filtered through the window over the sink. The back door was open, letting a cool breeze waft gently about the kitchen. I gasped as something brushed against my calf, then looked down to see a plump ginger cat with orb-like green eyes twisted around my legs. I laughed and tickled him behind the ears. He purred in delight. I settled into a chair at the table as Emmer made tea. I watched her thoughtfully, wondering what she was thinking.

Finally, she settled beside me. She demanded to know everything and I told her earnestly, hoping to God she would let me stay.

As I helped Emmer make dinner, the door slammed and in came my uncle Rory. Hair that was once blonde was now grey. Laughter lines creased his face like an old leather jacket. Shock flitted across his countenance as his eyes scrutinised my face. Then shock turned to sympathy. My father's temper wasn't a secret in the family. But each time a social worker would come, he would cover everything up and tell a big sob story about the hardships of having an 'ungrateful bratty teenager' to raise. He would feign shock, allowing it – as would a well-rehearsed actor – to consume his features when the social worker enquired about my neglect. I was too scared to tell the truth, even when my Dad wasn't there. After that, the most contact I had had with any other family member was when I would manage to scavenge from the bin a birthday card which they may have sent.

"Robyn," said Rory, nodding, his lips set in a grim line.

I smiled up at his weather-beaten face. I repeated my story for him. They both agreed that it would be best if I rested for the night before going to the Gardaí. Fear bubbled up inside me, as I contemplated how my father would react when he would come to realise that I had told the Gardaí.

My aunt was setting the table for dinner when the doorbell rang. My uncle flung down the paper he was reading and went out to the door. Suddenly, a crashing blow echoed down the hallway. I gasped as my father came thundering towards me, my uncle unconscious on the floor behind him.

"You!" he roared, outrage etched in his every feature. I felt the colour leave my face. Terror gripped me. He would surely kill me now.

"Dad," I tried to explain, but the word came out in a croaky whisper. I stood there frozen. I heard Emmer's blood-curdling scream, then all went black ...

# Her Story

## *Emma Waldron*

"NOW GIRLS, for English homework, I am assigning a writing exercise for each of you," announced the Principal, Mr. Johnson, in his monotonous voice.

"Ughh!" mumbled Sarah's classmates, droning in unison.

'Finally!' thought Sarah. Something to occupy her mind. She sat upright. For the last five minutes of class she eagerly listened to the story-writing assignment that was to be her English homework.

The bus ride home was filled with its normal complaints about homework.

"Did you see the homework Mr. Bloody Johnson gave us?!?"

"I know, right! For God's sake, like, and the goddamn Geography homework too!"

All Sarah could do was join in with the complainers. Happy as she was with the homework, she didn't want to seem weird.

Once home, Sarah was happily away from the whining voices of her all-too-negative peers and into the calm serenity that was her living-room couch. The theme music of 'Home and Away' and the troubled lives of the cast of 'Eastenders' occupied her mind, making her oblivious to any important matters she had to deal with.

It was 7:30pm when she tore her eyes from the television and started her homework. Maths, Irish, Geography and History, to name but a few of her subjects. 'Better leave English till last', she thought. 'It'll be easier to think of something'. But, oh, what a mistake that was!

8.30pm. She was almost finished her homework – nothing left but English.

"Sarah!" It was her mother.

"Yeah, Mom?"

"Are you finished your homework yet?"

"Almost. Just my English left."

"Well, hurry up, it's getting late!"

8.50pm. Still no sign of even an attempt at a story. After numerous trips to the kitchen to make some tea, Sarah realised that she was suffering from the dreaded writer's block.

"Shit, shit, shit," she muttered, trying to rattle her brain for evidence of an idea. But nothing. "It's okay, it's okay, it's okay. Just calm down and think," she advised herself aloud. But she was starting to worry.

9.15pm. Frustration etching at her brain. A pulling of her hair. Nails digging into her hands until droplets of blood formed. Nothing was working. And now she was hyperventilating. Tears were mounting in her eyes as her brother walked in.

"Ah, for Christ's sake, Sarah. Not again!"

"Screw off, Cian."

"No, Sarah! Why do you do this every time? It's just a story. Write something and go."

"I don't know what to bloody-well write! The stupid teacher didn't tell us what to do." Anger was building up inside her now, instinctively being directed at everyone except herself.

"Then don't write it, if you don't understand."

"I do bloody understand! But that damned Mr. Johnson told us to write about anything as long as we can fecking-well connect to it!"

Sarah blinked. Droplets of water hitting the still blank page.

"Why are you crying over a story?!?"

"Just get the hell out, Cian!" she screamed, pointing towards the door. And, as Cian stormed off, more tears fell. Tears on tears.

She reflected back on the start of the day, thinking that if she figured out how she got into this mess, she would be able to find a way out of it. From the moment she awoke, up until her History session – the class she had before English – nothing inspiring happened. She remembered that in English they had been studying an extract from 'To Kill a Mocking Bird' – nothing interesting there either. Then there was the homework Mr. Johnson had given them. He had told them to write about something they know, something they can connect to. Her mind skimmed through the events of the day. Up until the point her brother walked in, that is. How she felt as she was screaming at him seemed to catch her attention, the pent-up anger inside permeating her words. The rage, the frustration, the burning desire to throw something were memories now vivid in her mind.

Then suddenly, it hit. An idea. Inspiration.

9.45pm. Eventually she had started writing. Writing without thinking. Writing whilst thinking ahead. Venting emotion and creativity through her pen and then onto the page.

10.40pm. Relief melted its way throughout her body as she signed off on the last two words of her story: *'her story'*.

# Lifeless

## *James Hogan*

AARON STARED across the open ground from the cover of his foxhole. The light blanket of snow that covered the landscape had been thrown into the air by a bombardment of mortars. The barrage had gone on for quite some time now. A pause between the explosions allowed him to catch a glimpse of the body of his friend. It lay on the ground, lifeless. Aaron dragged himself from his foxhole onto the rough, debris-strewn surface of the earth. He struggled to his feet and steadily gained pace. In time, he allowed himself to stop and regain balance, then continued towards his comrade. Yet another mortar shell exploded behind him, the force jettisoning him onto the body of his friend.

"Buddy?" he cried, gasping for breath. No response. It was only then that he noticed a pool of blood surrounded him. His head filled with memories. Memories of boot camp. Memories of the war. The shock left him still, face down in the mud. Yet another explosion threw a shower of earth onto him, awakening him from his daze. He quickly rose to his feet, stumbling yet again. As he began to run for cover, the barrage stopped, bringing an end to the terror. He saw nothing for a few seconds, the dust in the air hampering his vision. Then, slowly settling onto the ground, the dust had disappeared. Aaron looked all around him. The ground was littered with the corpses of the men of his battalion. Ten, twenty – he didn't know how many. Limbs were scattered in various places, each in its own pool of blood. Then it hit him: he was all that was left. The only one alive in his whole battalion. He cried for help. No response.

Yet again he let out a shout, followed only by a deafening silence.

# The Morning Shift

## *Emmet O'Dwyer*

BEE-BEEP, BEE-BEEP, *bee-b–* I reach out, depress the On–Off button and roll onto my stomach.

"Six-thirty," I mumble disgruntedly, then swear into the pillow at the thought of facing Mr. O'Hara again after last weekend's mishap. Then I immediately feel the pounding of my head. Raising a hand to my forehead, I feel the teeming sweat. I groan in pain, put my feet out on the ground and stand. Out the bedroom door and over to the bathroom, almost falling over myself. As my feet hit the cold bathroom tiles, I shiver. Then, having finished my business, I return to my room. I take my pathetic excuse for a uniform out of the wardrobe and head downstairs.

As I leave my flat, a sudden burst of icy cold air hits me. My teeth chatter. I run to my car and hop in. The engine splutters when I turn the key.

"Not this again," I say, hitting my head against the car horn. Out I get and go around to the boot. The ice makes just opening the boot yet another hassle. Once opened, I take out the hammer and slam it shut again. Then up with the bonnet, a couple of taps on the engine, hop in, turn the key and, hey presto, off she goes!

At work I decide to use the drive-thru. I am starved to death, since I didn't have any breakfast. Ned is at the reception order window, his head pressed sleepily against the pane of glass. He jumps with fright as the car comes to a halt.

"Hey Ryan, what's up?" Ned asks, in a shaky voice, as he slides the window back.

"Nothing much," I say.

"Hey, aren't you working today?"

"Yep, but first I'm getting my breakfast."

"OK! So, may I have your order, please?"

"Well, I'll have a sausage burger with egg and some hash browns."

"Anything to drink with that?"

"No," I say, impatiently.

"Alrighty."

"Just get it all ready."

I park in the staff parking, then walk into the restaurant where my breakfast is ready on the counter. The smell of pork and egg puts a smile on my face. I grab it and drop myself down on one of the seats. I'm just about to take a bite out of a hash brown when I'm interrupted by Mr. O'Hara.

"What now?" I ask, while tossing my hash brown on the tray.

"You're late," says Mr. O'Hara.

"Yah, so?"

"Hey, lose the attitude," O'Hara says. "This is your third time being late."

"Cut me some slack, will you?"

"No. I will cut you some slack," he says, mimicking me, "if you start being more attentive around here. Now, throw that food in the bin and get to work."

"But –"

"No buts, young man. You are on very thin ice. I would change my attitude if I were you."

As he turns back to his office, I flip him the finger and get up to chuck my food in the bin. Hopping over the counter, I approach Ned.

"Don't you just hate working here, Ned?" I say.

"Nah, not really. He can be a jerk, but if you're on his good side, he's really nice."

I hear someone clear his throat and I turn around. It's Robert O'Bryan. Everyone who has worked here hates this little smart mouth. He is always making fun of staff about their uniforms and how pathetic their jobs are. Well, he has a point.

"Hey, gentlemen, how are you?" he asks, in that devious tone of his.

"What do you want?" I ask.

"Well, I'll have a …" He stops then, noticing Ned in the back of the kitchen.

Robert smiles, and I can see what is about to happen.

"Come over here," says Robert.

"Yes," replies Ned, somewhat sheepishly.

"God, Ned, you're still working here! What age are you? Twenty, twenty-one?"

"Twenty-four," replies Ned.

Robert starts laughing under his breath. "Wow, Ned! Twenty-four! And you're still flipping burgers, man! And I thought Ryan was bad."

"Hey, shut your mouth and just tell us what you want," I say.

"Well, I'll have a Big Mac and a Diet Coke."

"Any fries with that?" asks Ned, too afraid to say something back.

"No, I'll stick with that," says Robert.

I go into the kitchen and the thoughts of him abusing Ned go through my mind. Ned is a nice guy and nobody makes fun of him but me. I'm about to make Robert his food, then a devious plot comes to my mind. I sneak out to my car and grab my hammer from the boot of the car. I rush back in the backdoor, where Robert can't see me. I make his burger, pick out four flies from the fly trap and mash them into his burger with the hammer. I get some ice and put it in a cup. Then I make for the staff toilets and throw the ice into one of the urinals and scoop it back up. Walking to the counter with his spoiled grub, I can see the smug smile on his face.

"Wow, that was fast," said Robert.

"And fresh," I say, looking at him as he leaves. I try to keep a straight face. I watch him and see him taking a sip of his drink outside. I'm about to burst out laughing when Ned taps me on the shoulder.

"What did you do?" asks Ned.

"Nothing much," I say, half-laughing.

I glance at the clock above my head. 12:14. Yes! Only one hour to go, then I'm free and back home. Ned is already leaving work for the day. He has been here since four in the morning. He's just about to leave the kitchen when he takes a sudden tumble. I look at him, smirking.

"Where the hell did this come from?" he barks, as he gets up, holding my hammer.

"Oh, yeah, I was wondering where I put that," I say.

"An apology would be nice," Ned says, tossing the hammer on the counter and walking away. Lying back on one of the chairs, I yawn with exhaustion.

13:37. "If Josh doesn't show up, I'm going to freak," I say. O'Hara doesn't even give a hoot that my replacement has not shown up to relieve me from my shift.

"He should have been here ages ago," I shout, slamming my hand down on the counter.

"Will you be quiet! You're upsetting the customers," says O'Hara.

"Ah, screw that! Do you think I care about these snotty-nosed little brats?"

"Will you shut up. You're driving me mad," says O'Hara, and he paces up and down.

"Yeah, yeah, I have heard it all before."

"Mommy, why are the people shouting?" a little boy in the background asks.

"Can it, kid," I say.

"Excuse me!" rasps his mother.

O'Hara grabs me by the scruff of the neck and drags me to his office.

"What do you think you are doing, talking to a four year-old like that?"

"Oh, and what are *you* doing treating me like dirt? You think you're above me, yeah? I'm only 19 and I'm just working here for a couple of months, but you're in your forties, maybe even fifties, and you're a manager in a fast food joint! God, get a grip, will ya! An eight year-old could do that."

"You!" says O'Hara.

"Just leave it there, O'Hara. I'm out of here." I burst out of his office and see the kid crying.

"You can't leave," says O'Hara, following me to the car.

"No! Well, you just watch me."

I get in the car and slam the door. O'Hara just stands there looking at me, not knowing what to do. And I take off.

I'm on the main road and thinking about what I said to O'Hara. His gobsmacked look brings a smile to my face. Then the engine splutters. "Ah, damn it!" I say, rolling my eyes to the heavens.

I pull over, get out of the car and go around to the boot to get my hammer. It's not in there. I check the front seat of the car and still no hammer. Then it hits me like a ton of bricks. It's back on the reception counter.

# Enough

## *Jane Fitzpatrick*

**Monday, 11th December**

"Watch where you're walking, loser. Move."

I am jeered, even while walking into school. It is constant, persistent, endless.

Over a year of it now and still no sign of it letting up. The bathroom, cafeteria, art room – Games is the worst. I just can't go anywhere. They rule my life. My friends, my happiness, my sense of self-belonging, they have all gone. It's not as if my 'friends' now have anything against me, but no one wants to get on the wrong side of Katie. And as for school – I feel sick every morning and every night when I think about it. But not for the reasons you might think. God, I love tests – anything even related to staying in class under the watchful eye of the teacher. Some bits, though, I feel as other people feel. The talks infuriate me, particularly the ones about bullying: 'Don't be afraid to tell a trusted parent or friend. They'll handle it from there'.

Yeah, we all know what that means. Like that is even a possibility. Like they have contemplated, or even can contemplate, what would happen to me if I told. I've been given the outline myself. Oh, people suspect what is going on alright. The teachers, for instance: how my grades jumped from 60 to 100 the very same time that the circle of friends around me disappeared; how I spend the full 40 minutes eating my lunch at a table by myself; how they see me crying in the corner of the classroom. And my parents: how I never leave the house, apart from school and piano; how they constantly ask me to have a friend down; how they have to pull me out of bed weeping every morning.

**Tuesday, 12th December**

What can I say? Just a week ago my teacher, Ms. O'Neill, told me to keep this diary.

"Isabelle," – sigh – "you won't tell me anything, so at least write it down. You can't keep everything bottled up."

So, here I am, doing it. It has gotten worse. I was in the bathroom – I just couldn't put it off anymore – and Annabel and her gang were discussing some disco or other, and then, out of the blue, she turned to me and asked, "Are you going, Isabelle?" I was shocked. It had been 50 weeks since Annabel has spoken to me. Annabel, who used to be my best friend. I was just getting over her asking and preparing to answer when Katie jumped in and, with one of those looks she reserves for me, she struck, "No, no, she isn't." Then she saw Annabel staring, her eyebrows raised.

"Em, you have something on that day, don't you, Isabelle?" said Katie. She looked at me. I had to nod. What choice did I have? What choice do I ever have?

**Wednesday, 13th December**

I don't know if I can take this anymore.

**Thursday, 14th December**

Just back from the hospital. Mom saw my face and completely over-reacted. Katie found this diary, this stupid diary where I idiotically wrote what they have been doing to me. I brought it in my bag to school – the DUMBEST thing, without doubt, that I have ever done. I was going to show it to Ms. O'Neill. I was at her door, about to knock, when my bag split and books, pens and my lunch were all over the ground, and – *the diary*. Katie was passing, of course, and, knowing the size of a diary and recognising the unmistakable stupid pink shiny cover, a look of apprehension crossed her ugly face. She picked it up, opened and read, 'Watch where you're walking, loser'. Her eyes skimmed down the page to 'No one wants to get on the wrong side of Katie'. Anger mounted and her face became a blotchy red colour. She put two and two together. Me. Ms. O'Neill's door. The diary. Losing it completely, she lashed out at me, hitting and scraping at my face, punching my stomach and grabbing my legs, so that I whacked my head off the tile floor. I screamed. Ms. O'Neill stirred inside and was moving closer and closer to the door.

"Shut up!" Katie hissed, furiously, then dragged me by the legs to the jacket closet. "Now you just think about what you nearly did," she barked, then shut the door and locked me in. I was left there until 5 o'clock this evening, when my Mom came to the school looking for me. She found me after about a half hour of panicked shouting. I couldn't answer her. My mouth was full of my own blood. She burst into tears when she saw me. "Oh, Izzy, who did this to you?" I wouldn't answer. I know I won't have to put up with it anymore.

### Friday, 15th December

Friday night. It's cold. It's dark. The ropes are hanging. Even from where I'm standing, my view and the state my life is in, it looks like a very painful thing, but I can't put up with this anymore. I just can't. I'll miss my family, sure. And they will miss me. And my sisters – I'm sorry, I love you but I just can't, I can't …

"A report from our correspondent, Samantha Librari, who is in the city centre."

*"Gardaí have reported that the body of a fourteen year-old girl was found here in the gym of the St. Calasanctus Secondary School for Girls earlier this evening. Though not yet conclusive, indications are that she has taken her own life and Gardaí have confirmed that, at this point, they are not seeking any other party in the matter. We understand that a journal, detailing incidents of bullying which the young girl suffered, along with a note to her family were found by her body …"*

# The Memory

## Seán Reddan

***The Memory:*** The two boys sped around the corner and eyed the finish line, some forty metres away. The younger of the two, Gerry, was only barely holding on to first place, as had been the case throughout. Liam's face oozed frustration. He claimed to be the better racer, but that very much remained to be seen. Initially, the race was a bit of fun, as the roads were icy and the quads would drift brilliantly, if handled correctly. But, as the race wore on, Liam realised his pride was on the line. He saw a very icy patch on the road straight ahead of him, very close to the finish line. He sped up and moved over a little to the right of the younger boy. As the front wheels of Gerry's quad drove over the ice, the older boy moved in and gave his competitor's quad a push to the left. He had timed it well and, as all the weight moved to the back of Gerry's quad, the front wheels slid helplessly off the ice and put the other boy in first place. Perfect. His handling was very good. Gerry accelerated in order to straighten himself out and possibly get himself back in front. But that only made the situation worse. The raw force pushed Gerry's quad into the wall. On impact, Gerry jammed his leg between the quad and the stone facade. An instant break. Then his body whiplashed and, as he fell back over, the broken bone ripped through his calf.

Liam was oblivious to his comrade's desperate screams for help. He only looked back when he was well across the finish line.

***The Now:*** Liam sits uncomfortably as the two guards enter the questioning room. Though he is trying very hard to keep calm, he is mindful of his ever-growing nervousness.

"Good morning, Mr. Fitzhenry," says the female guard.

"Good morning," Liam replies. He notices that his voice is smooth. He thinks he can do this.

"As you know, we've asked you to come in today in relation to the death of Gerry Tuohy," says the male officer. Liam nods. He is getting increasingly nervous.

"How are you?" asks the female guard.

"Fine, thank you."

"Have you been sleeping well the last few days?"

"Yeah, good."

The male guard immediately jots down his reply. Liam feels he shouldn't have lied to this question.

"We believe you were with Gerry at the time of his death," the female officer says.

"Yes."

"Can you tell us what happened, please?"

"OK! Well, Gerry and I met up at the local pitch for a game of soccer. We always played on a Friday evening. There was a light frost, but it didn't matter. We were wrapped up, so we didn't feel cold. We usually walked back to his house after the game. But it was getting dark, so we went to my house, which is just outside the village. Then we drove to his house from there on my quad."

Liam's voice is still calm at this point. He continues. "Gerry only got his new quad bike three weeks earlier, a 250cc farming quad. The power of it was unreal. He suggested we have a race. I wanted to go inside, but he was already backing his quad out of the garage. I said OK. I gave in, but I've never regretted anything so much."

Liam feels he is convincing the guards. But the reality is that it was he who really wanted to race in the first place.

"We decided we would race to the tennis court, about 400 metres away, then back again. We set down two blocks, which were to be the start and finish line. The corner was icy and this concerned us both momentarily."

"So, why did you go ahead with the race when you were aware of the danger?" the male guard asked.

"We thought we could drift it. We were in situations like this before," said Liam.

Once the male guard had written this down, he invited Liam to continue.

"Gerry got a lucky start. His quad was really fast, so I guess I was about four seconds behind him. He had turned the corner for the finish line as I was at the halfway point. Just as I had turned the corner for the finish line, I saw him flying off his quad. He broke his leg really badly. It was horrible. He was dead when I got to him. There was nothing I could do."

And, with that, Liam puts his head down. He waits for one of the guards to say something. But the only noise is the scratching of the tip of the male officer's pen against the paper.

"Thank you, Liam," says the female officer. "I'm sure this has been very upsetting for you, but your information is very helpful to us." Then the guards rise and leave the room.

*The Future*: As the quad nears its top speed, Liam thinks one last time about his best friend. The lies have haunted him ever since the questioning, almost four months ago. Waking up in a cold sweat night after night. It was all too much. He will end it once and for all. He is not scared as the approaching car comes closer and closer.

# Sniper

## *Ruádhan Slevin*

ALL IS CALM as the village lies blanketed in snow. Suddenly, the silence is disturbed by the crackling of a radio coming from the top of an abandoned church tower. Sitting in the corner of the tower, trying to keep himself warm, is the lone figure of a French rebel sniper, who has taken refuge in the building these past three days. As he listens closely to the device, trying to catch up on the latest news of the war, he dares not raise the volume for fear of being heard. He is a member of the local French Resistance.

When the German Infantry attacked the village, they ravaged the houses and killed defenceless home owners without a thought. They were not human, thought the sniper to himself. He had tried to defend his home from the advancing troops, but he quickly realised that this was a fight he could not win. There were simply too many of them. The planes flew overhead, dropping their payload on the buildings below, causing mayhem. Fire spread through the village, forcing its occupants to flee onto the streets, only to be met by a hail of gunfire from the insurgents.

The rebel had witnessed every bit of this. But, instead of standing up to these oppressors who had taken his home, fear overtook him and he turned his back on his kin and duty, and ran away. He had taken cover atop the church tower. Luckily, he was not spotted as he climbed the seemingly endless staircase. He had found a sheltered space, surrounded by carved stone pillars. The room was small, dark and from the ceiling hung the church bell. The walls had carvings of holy saints and religious moments in history. Somehow, it all brought the rebel peace. And the days passed …

He has been in cover for a long time now. It has been torture for him, not knowing what has befallen his family and friends. He thinks himself a coward, running away from battle as he has done – he who has been trained to stare death in the face. He has shamed his country.

As he crouches in the tower, he occasionally takes a peek out through the space between the pillars of the structure. Risky as it may seem, it is the only way to see if he is safe. As he looks across the one-time peaceful, but now lifeless village, the whiteness of the snow does battle with the blackness of the night sky. Memories of his childhood flood back into his mind. He remembers running through the streets, playing games with his friends, causing trouble. He smiles at the thought.

But memories are soon wiped away as the black sky is suddenly filled with the bright orange reflection of a raging fire. The houses across from the tower have been hit. The ground shakes with the impact of successive shells and fire has spread voraciously. It dances up against the dark of night, bringing light into the sky. They have ravaged his village, his family and friends. Grief has stricken him. The rebel rummages in his pockets and finally pulls out his tobacco, thinking that a smoke might help. Rolling up the white paper, he returns to his pockets for his lighter. The risk of being seen is the last thought running through his head. The light momentarily fills the tower and then it's gone. He draws long and slowly on the cigarette, the smoke seeming to relax him. But relaxation is short-lived. Soon, bullets are piercing the pillars of the tower, some coming perilously close to him. As fear mounts, the memories of grief sweep over him anew. He draws his weapon from his back holster and aims slowly and determinedly at his enemy. Running is not an option.

# Blue Canoe

## *Rachel Flanagan*

THE MOMENT I SEE THE HOUSE I hate it. It's an inexplicable feeling. There should be no reason for me to have such strong feelings for a house I have never set eyes on before. I suppose you could even call it beautiful. It's a typical New England clapboard house, two stories high and probably a couple of hundred years old, nestled into a deep and majestic oak forest. It's in surprisingly good condition too, although the garden – completely overgrown with climbing roses and nettles – leaves a lot to be desired. I can already see the hours of enjoyment my parents are going to get out of this. It'll be another one of their 'projects' and, no doubt, I will be doomed to spend my entire summer weeding the garden and painting the dingy clapboard. This ought to be good.

I climb out of the car, legs aching from the four and a half hour-long car journey from New York to our new house. It is set just a few miles south of Holliston, Massachusetts. I stand back and gaze up at the house, strangely feeling a sudden and overwhelming sense of loneliness and isolation. Ever-mindful of all that I have left behind, I reach into my pocket and, for the umpteenth time, open the tear-stained letter from my school friends.

*'Dear Rebecca,'*, it reads, *'we will always miss you and hope you won't forget all of us here in New York! Promise we'll visit as soon as we can. Good luck in your new home (surely the countryside won't be as bad as you think it will). Much love.'*

I repress the tears welling up behind my eyes. I have to put on a brave face for my parents and hope that somehow I'll be able to adjust to this whole upheaval.

Later that day, I decide to explore my new surroundings. My face is aching from pretending to smile all morning, while we unpacked the car and tried to settle into the new house. I just need to go away and sulk for a while. So, I head off into the woods, following a trail which I suppose will lead me to the lake that is mentioned in the brochure we were given by the real estate agent.

After about ten minutes of stumbling over rocks and tangled roots, I finally emerge out of the undergrowth and onto the banks of a lake. The water is incredibly clear and it glistens in the afternoon sunshine. It's idyllic, really – circular and surrounded on all sides by woodland. Willows dip their leaves along the water's edge. There are glittering dragonflies humming over the glassy surface of the lake and everything seems so peaceful. Somehow, however, I still feel uneasy, as if someone is watching from the dappled shade of the trees behind me. Walking a little further along the water's edge, I notice a small wooden jetty jutting out among the reeds, and a little wooden boathouse, which I almost miss for a moment because it is so dilapidated. On closer inspection, I find an old canoe tied to the jetty with some frayed rope. It is partly submerged, so that only the stern, with its peeling blue paint, is visible. It all feels not quite right. The boathouse is empty, but there is an ominous atmosphere and a heavy, damp, musty smell hanging in the air. I decide that I've seen enough for now.

Reluctantly, I make my way back to the house. It certainly doesn't feel like home, despite the inviting and familiar smell of Mom's homemade lasagne wafting out of the windows as I approach.

Dinnertime conversation is awkward. My parents are desperately trying to elicit some enthusiasm from me.

"So, what do you think, Becky? It's wonderful, isn't it!" Mom exudes, beaming eagerly at me.

"Yeah, it's nice, I guess …"

"Your room is lovely. I'm thinking of painting it forget-me-not blue, to go with those lovely curtains I bought last year and the

121

quilt your Grandmother gave you for your birthday. What do you think, honey?"

"Mmm …" My mouth being full saves me from having to look too interested. After a while, Mom gives up and we lapse back into a melancholic silence.

That night, I sleep badly. The moon is pouring through my uncurtained windows and there is a strange unearthly silence here that is unlike anything I have ever experienced. I'm used to the constant sound of traffic sirens and the garishness of neon city lights lulling me to sleep. But the quietness here almost hurts my ears. It is only broken once in a while by the chirping of crickets or the screech of an owl. Occasionally, during the night, the house creaks. It is almost as if it is breathing.

The morning sunshine literally sheds a new light on the room. I drag myself out of bed – more tired now than I was when I got in last night – and begin to unpack the large cardboard boxes piled in the corner of the otherwise empty room. My furniture is packaged up in the hallway, waiting to be hauled into my room. I set into the task. The process doesn't take long. I have a mirror, a chest of drawers and a bedside table. I haven't got very many clothes or personal belongings. There's a scrapbook from my old friends, my CD collection and low-tech sound system, a musical box that I was given for my 7th birthday and my sketching stuff. Besides that, there is very little else. The room still looks empty, especially with its stark white-painted walls and woodwork. My window overlooks the back garden. And I also have a clear view of the boathouse and the lake, which is strange because they seemed so hidden when I stumbled upon them.

I give myself a tour of the rest of the house. There is a long empty corridor outside my room, with several doors leading off it. One of these belongs to my parents. I have absolutely no idea why they bought such a large house when there are only three of us. My door is opposite the staircase. The newel posts are tall and rounded at the top, and remind me slightly of blank-faced sentries standing guard, watching and waiting for something. The rest of the house has a similar layout and the colour scheme is uniform throughout the building – lots of off-whites, grey-blue tones and painted woodwork. The floorboards are obviously ancient. They creak and sigh with every movement I make. There is very little furniture in the house, except for a mirror with a tarnished silver frame in the upstairs corridor and a dusty old sideboard downstairs in the dining room.

That night, before I go to bed, I go in to say goodnight to my parents.

"Dad, do you know anything about the boathouse down at the lake?"

"Well, I'm pretty sure that it was part of the deal when we bought this house, Becky. Perhaps we can fix it up a bit and get a little boat over the summer. I've heard the lake is very good for fishing."

I nod and give him a kiss, before making my way up the stairs to my room. On the halfway landing, the newel posts stare forebodingly down at me. I reach the top of the stairs, then glance down the corridor to my left. Suddenly, the hairs rise on the back of my neck. I get the distinct impression that someone, or something, is standing at the end of the hallway. It's a dark shadow, and because I'm so incredibly tired, I can't be sure whether my eyes are playing tricks on me or not. When I blink, it's gone. I dismiss it. Time for bed.

My screams pierce the night. I waken, trembling, damp with sweat, feverish from the nightmare. My parents come rushing into my room.

"Rebecca, Rebecca! What's wrong?" My Mom cradles me in her arms and strokes my hair. There are harsh, rasping, uncontrollable sobs coming from my throat. The noises barely seem to be my own.

"Nightmare …" I pant, in between more violent sobs. My parents exchange worried glances.

In the morning, as I am dressing, I notice a series of rough gashes along the top of my shoulder. They are red and raw, and clearly new. I search my bed frantically for some sharp object that might have caused them. There is nothing. No protruding mattress springs or stray nails. If it weren't so ridiculous, it would appear as though some strange bird of prey had scratched me. I try to remember what I dreamed about. I can't.

It's been almost a week since the scratches. They are all but healed now. This morning, I waken to find my fingernails encrusted in a reddish-brown substance. It smells metallic. I assume that it is rust. I go for a walk to the boathouse. I feel drawn there for some reason that I can't explain. The lake looks murkier today, despite the glowing sunshine. I decide to drag the canoe out of the reeds and inspect in. The structure still seems to be good, but for a couple of small holes drilled into the wood, which I presume to be what has caused its submergence among the cat's-tail reeds. I want to repair it. It would be quite attractive if I fixed it up and maybe gave it a new coat of paint, or planted flowers in it. Perhaps it can be my summer project and a good excuse to stay out of my parents' way while they work on restoring the new house.

I make a disturbing discovery later in the day. There is a dead sparrow on my windowsill. A long steel nail pushed through its chest. The feathers are sticky with congealed blood. How did it get there? I'm not going to tell my parents about this. It might upset them. I now realise that it was not rust on my fingernails this morning …

It's raining tonight. I can hear the distant rolls of thunder and see the lightning illuminate my room every so often. I hope this means that the heat will subside a little now.

Another day. I spend my time working on the canoe down at the boathouse. I find a tin of blue paint in one of the cupboards. I suppose that it's the paint that Mom intended to use in my room.

I'm sure she won't miss it. Anyway, she's too busy with her various DIY jobs.

The lake is calm today, but ominous. I wonder, vaguely, how deep it is. The crystalline waters look quite dark and dense near the centre. Yes, but how time passes here …

And yet another day has come and gone. I'm afraid to go to sleep tonight. I don't want to go back to my room, so I put off bedtime for as long as possible, watching a movie with my parents. It's a ridiculous romantic comedy. The plot is so boring and predictable that I soon doze off on the sofa.

I dream. Someone calls me. A woman's voice. It is very soft and seems somewhat muffled. I see her emerge from the shadows, smiling, beckoning to me. In the distance I can hear screams and odd splashing noises.

I awaken. Bright white sunlight streams through my eyelids. I can hear birds chirping, reeds rustling, water lapping. I sit up and stretch. My surroundings are unfamiliar. Rough, wooden, whitewashed walls. Light filtering through the many cracks. My bare feet are full of splinters. The Boathouse! A sense of dread fills me. What is happening to me?

For the next three mornings, I wake outside in the garden. And, on yet another morning, on the decayed jetty by the lake. I lock my door at night, but I still end up leaving my bed.

Someone has been in my room. Today, my entire CD collection was strewn across the floor, each one shattered into pieces. I'm trying so hard to pretend that everything is normal, but it's getting difficult. I think my parents are starting to suspect that something is wrong.

In the afternoon, I finish painting the outside of the canoe. The sun is scorching and sweat rolls off me in tiny beads. I'll give it a second coat tomorrow. I lie down among the reeds and enjoy the cool restful shade. Today, I don't feel uncomfortable here. All is quiet and tranquil by the lake. Water beetles and little toads frolic in the warm still water, weaving between the blossoming water lilies. Willow trees dance on the river bank. Grasshoppers chirp from the shade of the trees.

Later, as I am walking back to the house, I look up at my room. It's hard to tell from a distance, but I think that someone is standing in my window. When I ask Mom if she was in there, she says no. That's not the answer I was hoping for.

Another night, another morning. There are more scratches, this time on my back. A day passes filled with worry, and I fear the darkness and falling asleep. What will tonight bring? Tiredness forces a surrender. To bed. To sleep … eventually.

Down the stairs. The front door is open, moonlight pooling onto the floor. She is waiting for me. Her hair is long, dark and slimy, like the water weeds that line the lake's edge. I will follow her. I walk down beyond the garden's edge, feet catching on briars and stones. Through the forest, leaves and branches brush my face. Amongst water reeds, then into murky shallows. The canoe is there, bobbing peacefully in the moonlight, beckoning. I climb in, forgetting about the tiny holes that I never plugged. I push off from the bank, trailing my fingers through the silver moonlit water, then look back. She is standing on the bank among the reeds, smiling as the water fills the canoe. And I slip into the swirling black depths.

# Author Profiles

*Clare County Library requested of the participants that they each write a very short reflection on the value of this course in creative writing to them. Brief profiles, each with the respective writer's comment, are given below.*


**Rebecca Austin**, *An Oíche* (St. Patrick's Comprehensive School, Shannon)
Rebecca was 16 at the time of taking this course and was then in Transition Year. She is currently studying Politics and Public Administration at the University of Limerick. Rebecca writes, swims and continues with sign language, which she took up at the same time as commencing the creative writing course with Ré. She also has a keen interest in politics and good debate.

> *"The course was a chance to pursue an interest which, in turn, became a hobby. Ré brought a whole new dimension to my writing, allowing me to write in a way I never could have imagined."*


**Oisín Bates**, *No Parking* (St. Patrick's Comprehensive School, Shannon)
Aged 17 when participating in the course, Oisín was a 5th Year student who has now gone on to study English and History at the University of Limerick. Oisín still writes and is an avid reader, his favourite author being John Steinbeck, through whose novels he is steadily making his way. He has an interest in modern history and attempts to play saxophone and guitar, though, to quote him, 'I am closer to the Ringo Starr side of the performer's spectrum'.

> *"The workshops were of significance to me, as nothing of their kind had been previously available to me during my time in school. Ré was a great character. The vibrancy of his personality had a great effect in stimulating the group's interaction and creativity. I really appreciated the effort of Clare County Library (and, especially for us, its Shannon branch) in facilitating such a programme. Thanks for everything."*

**Lanci Marshall Borota**, *Silent Grace* (St. Caimin's Community School, Shannon)
Lanci was a 16 year-old Junior Cert student at the time of taking the course. She has since returned home to the United States and is currently studying International Law at Monmouth College in Monmouth, Illinois. Lanci's greatest passion is riding ponies and horses. She has particularly enjoyed the hunt in Ireland and, equally so, her show ring jumping in the mountains of Colorado. She is adamant that 'writing is and always will be part of my soul'.

> *"It was such an honour to be chosen for the workshop with Ré. He had such a respectful way of boosting my confidence. Young writers need a brilliant guide to open new ways of writing, and I was granted this gift in Ré Ó Laighléis. Thank you."*

**Joe Brown**, *Justice* (Ennistymon Vocational School)
Joe took the course when in 5th Year. He was then 17 years-old. At the time of publication, he will have completed his Leaving Certificate. Joe loves scuba-diving, which is what provided the backdrop for his story – 'It's beautiful down there', he tells us. For relaxation, he enjoys a good book, his favourite author currently being Peter F. Hamilton. His latest hobby, and one more likely related to his book reading than to scuba-diving (though, who knows?), is amateur wine-making.

> *"I believe that the course was very beneficial to my writing skills and having Ré as an adviser and editor helped me to refine my writing style. Having my story being read publicly assured me that my writing skills were good enough to be exposed to others. Ré also had a great sense of humour and I never felt like the sessions were great labours, because the mood was kept light."*

**Sophie Cassidy**, *Predator* (St. Patrick's Comprehensive School, Shannon)
Sophie, who is now a student at the University of Limerick, was a 17 year-old in her Leaving Certificate year at the time of taking the course. Sophie likes to write, play guitar, sketch and travel. She has a particular interest in the arts, languages and other cultures.

*"The course taught me a lot about myself, my strengths and creative writing in general. Besides that, it was fantastic to hear others' ideas and inspirations. The course was well-structured, well-taught and highly motivational."*

**Jaden Creagh**, *Eccentricity* (Kilrush Community School)

Jaden was a 14 year-old 1st Year student when he participated in the course. He is still a student in Kilrush Community School. He likes to read and write – he is currently in the early stages of writing his first book. His main hobby, however, is the assembly and painting of warhammer models.

*"The course was very enjoyable and Ré was a fantastic tutor. He was open-minded and encouraged my creativity. The course gave me the tools to write a good short story, but Ré gave me the confidence to write in a genre with which I felt comfortable."*

**Keelan Cunningham**, *Scouted* (Kilrush Community School)

Still attending Kilrush Community School, Keelan was a 13 year-old 1st Year student when he took this course. Most of Keelan's free time is spent on the playing field. He is an extremely keen footballer, as might be garnered from the theme of his story, *Scouted*. Other hobbies include music and, 'of course' (his words), writing.

*"I found the workshop significantly improved my creative writing. The techniques I learned have been a great asset to me when dredging through previously tedious English homework. The short story option in the Junior Certificate exam became all the more appealing with the skills that Ré had passed on to me. I would happily recommend this workshop to any post-primary student."*

**Jim Downes**, *The Death Penalty* (St. Joseph's Community College, Kilkee)

Jim was a 15 year-old 4th Year student when he participated in the course. He is now studying for a Bachelor of Education degree at Mary Immaculate College, Limerick. Jim has a great interest in football and plays at Minor and Intermediate levels with his local club O'Curry's. He also has a keen interest in soccer, rugby, golf and squash.

*"I found the course excellent as it gave me a way, finally, to structure my writing and it also helped me at the time to prepare for my Leaving Certificate exam."*

**Jane Fitzpatrick**, *Enough* (Kilrush Community School)
A 13 year-old and in 1st Year when she took the course, Jane is still a student at Kilrush Community School. She plays piano and concertina, and is also an avid reader. She would like to indulge in many more activities, but finds her eagerness for them somewhat tempered by the demands of homework.

*"I found the course to be extremely helpful in every aspect of my English studies. It helps with my essay writing, functional writing and, of course, story writing. I found Ré to be a very good writer and enjoyed his stories, which he kindly gave to us. I have put the many useful phrases and tips he gave us to good use and will hopefully continue to do so. English has always been my favourite subject in school and I find it all the more enjoyable now with the many tips and tricks shown to us by an experienced writer."*

**Rachel Flanagan**, *Blue Canoe* (Scoil Mhuire, Ennistymon)
Rachel was 16 and in Transition Year when she participated in the Ennistymon leg of the course. At time of going to print, she is still a student at Scoil Mhuire. She loves to paint, dance, read and write.

*"I really enjoyed the course and felt that it was incredibly useful, both for creative writing in and outside of school. It helped me to develop an interest in creative writing for personal enjoyment and it gave me the necessary techniques to do so."*

**Killian Geaney**, *Collapse* (St. Joseph's Community College, Kilkee)
Then 16 and a 4th Year student, Killian is currently studying for a Bachelor of Arts degree at the National University of Ireland, Galway. He has a keen interest in both playing and watching all types of sport. Despite the demands of a heavy college schedule and holding down a part-time job, he enjoys running and does so several times a week.

*"I found the course hugely beneficial as I was progressing through school and college. It gave me huge motivation when studying for my Leaving Cert and has helped me gain confidence during my studies in college. Many thanks to Ré."*

**James Hogan**, *Lifeless* (Ennistymon Vocational School)
James, who was 14 when he participated in the course, was then a 2nd Year student. He still attends Ennistymon Vocational School. James' hobbies include drawing (mostly sketches of familiar fictional characters and objects), fishing, football and occasionally going out with friends. He has an immense interest in graphic design and history. One day, he hopes to pursue a career in aviation or architecture.

*"An exceptionally joyous experience, which taught me a lot about writing a great story."*

**Amanda Honan**, *Night-time* (St. Joseph's Community College, Kilkee)
Amanda was 14 and in Junior Cert when she took this course. At the time of going to print, she will have completed her Leaving Certificate studies. Amanda loves to write. Art, artists and all creative endeavour fascinate her. She is an avid reader and an eager conversationalist. In keeping with family tradition, Amanda has embraced the art of oarsmanship and engages in currach racing. And, to cap it all off, she is an enthusiastic kickboxer.

*"I found the course hugely beneficial and I still use the skills I learned today. It was brilliant and I am very grateful for having had the opportunity to take part in it."*

**Alanagh Hunt**, *Intuition* (St. Caimin's Community College, Shannon)
Alanagh, who is now a student of Psychology and Sociology at the University of Limerick, was a 16 year-old 4th Year student when she took part in the course. She is ebullient and outgoing in nature and, as part of a charity drive, has recently learned and competed in ballroom dancing. She is also a part-time model and has a great interest in education.

*"I reminisce quite fondly on the workshop that I attended with Ré during school. He mustered great interest in me in creative writing and also nurtured my ability to develop creative writing skills. I feel that the course gave a new edge to my writing abilities."*

**Sam Kenyon**, *The Way of War* (Kilrush Community School)
Sam was 12 years of age and in 1st Year when he was a participant in the course. He is still a student at Kilrush Community School. Sam has eclectic taste, involving himself in soccer, basketball, Gaelic football, reading, video games and airsofting, the last of which he tells us is 'like paintballing, but with plastic pellets'.

*"The course was very informative. It taught me a lot about story structuring and story writing in general. I would definitely do the course again and encourage anyone who had the opportunity to take it."*

**Tara Mallon**, *Gone* (St. Caimin's Community School, Shannon)
Tara is currently studying Applied Languages at the University of Limerick. She was 16 when she took the course and a 4th Year student. Tara loves travelling, learning about different cultures and improving her languages. Music – listening to and concert-going – is another of her great joys, as is reading.

*"I thought the workshop was a fantastic experience. It gave me an insight into the thought and hard work that goes into producing a short story. It also helped me to develop my own skills as a writer. I think that I am benefiting from this course even in my current studies, as I am much more capable of viewing my work from a critical angle."*

**Alice Marr**, *Disconnect* (Scoil Mhuire, Ennistymon)
Alice was 16 and in Transition Year when she attended the course. She is currently pursuing her Leaving Certificate studies. Alice's interests are mainly in the area of the arts – art itself, as well as literature and music. 'I love contemporary dance and yoga, as well as singing and participating in theatrical performances', she tells us.

*"The course gave me an insight into the complexity of short story writing and all the creativity that is required to become a successful writer."*

**Michael McInerney**, *Release* (Meánscoil na mBráithre, CBS Ennistymon)
Michael was a 16 year-old Transition Year student when he participated in the course. As this goes to print, he is in his final year in secondary school and preparing for his Leaving Cert. Michael loves reading, which is, he says, what 'lead me to this course'. He also enjoys Playstation 3 and other consoles.

> *"The course was absolutely brilliant. Having the opportunity to be mentored by and work with a writer of Ré's calibre was fantastic. I feel my writing has improved and hope to use the skills I have learned in my Leaving Certificate."*

**Ciarán Morrissey**, *Rivalry* (Meánscoil na mBráithre, CBS Ennistymon)
Ciarán, who is currently studying for his Leaving Certificate, was 15 and in Transition Year when he took part in the course. His hobbies are football and farming. He plays for Kilmurry Ibrickane and is involved at Minor, Under-21, Intermediate and Senior levels. He also enjoys helping his father on his dairy farm of 24 cows.

> *"The course was extremely enjoyable and worthwhile. It will prove to be very useful to me during the Leaving Certificate and has given me a new-found interest in English. I would like to thank Ré for his efforts."*

**Laura Mulqueen**, *Get Away* (Kilrush Community School)
Laura was 15 years-old and in Junior Cert when she participated in the course. When this is published, she will have completed her Leaving Certificate studies. Laura enjoys browsing around a good bookstore whenever she visits a new town or city. She also enjoys writing short stories, meeting up with friends and going to the cinema.

> *"I think that this course really enhanced my creative writing skills. I feel more confident when writing, as my knowledge of writing styles is broader."*

**Dearbhla Edwards Murphy**, *Truth* (Kilrush Community School)
Dearbhla, who was 13 at the time of taking the course, was then a 1st Year student. She still attends Kilrush Community School. She is passionate about art and music, both of which she studies in school. She loves to draw and to play guitar and concertina (but not all at the one time!). She is very interested in languages, especially Irish and French. In her spare time, she likes to read and has a particular love for the classics of Brontë and Dickens.

> *"The course wasn't like I had anticipated. The friendly vibe of the class put me at ease and was hugely encouraging. The course gave me the confidence to not only write short stories, but many other writing compositions. Thanks for the opportunity."*

**Maria Murphy**, *Penalty* (Kilrush Community School)
Maria, who was a 15 year-old 5th Year student when she participated in the course, is currently studying Medicine at the National University of Ireland, Galway. Maria's hobbies are many and varied. She has a great interest in sports -- basketball, swimming, but most particularly Gaelic football. She is very involved with her local team, Kilrush Ladies Football Club, where she both plays and enjoys coaching the younger age groups. Maria also loves playing music, revelling in taking time out to learn a new piece for the piano.

> *"I found the course very enjoyable and it was very useful for my English in Leaving Cert."*

**Conor Murray**, *Shoot Out* (St. Joseph's Community College, Kilkee)
Conor was aged 15 and in Junior Cert when he attended the course. At the time of readying this book for publication, he is in his final year and preparing for his Leaving Certificate exams. Conor is a keen footballer, playing both for his club and for his school's Senior team. He likes to design and make objects from wood and metal, and, in this regard, enjoys working with his Dad, Paddy, particularly in creative metal fabrication, all of which complements his choice of areas of study – Construction, Design and Communications Graphics, as well as Engineering Studies. Other hobbies include reading and writing in both English and Gaeilge.

*"I really enjoyed the six-week course as I felt it truly improved my writing skills. Ré was fully dedicated each week, correcting each draft where necessary. I learned about the various aspects of short story writing and this has driven me on to write many more stories since."*

**James O'Connor**, *Forever in Time* (St. Patrick's Comprehensive School, Shannon)
James was 16 at the time of the course and was in 4th Year. Since then, he has completed his Leaving Cert and is currently studying HPSS (History, Politics, Sociology and Social Studies) at the University of Limerick. James' major hobbies are reading and going out with friends. He is also hugely engaged by politics and history, which interests dovetail well with his areas of study.

*"The course provided me with writing skills which I have retained and still use today. These skills of storytelling and editing were invaluable and unique to this course. I found it rewarding to see the finished story at the end of the process and it was a very good opportunity to work with a skilled and accomplished author."*

**Emmet O'Dwyer**, *The Morning Shift* (St. Patrick's Comprehensive School, Shannon)
Emmet was in 2nd Year and 14 years-old when he took part in the course. He is still a student at St. Patrick's Comprehensive School and is working towards his Leaving Certificate. Writing remains a hobby of Emmet's. He is also interested in history and the arts, and has a particular interest in film and other media.

*"The course was a great learning experience. It grabbed my attention with regard to the skills required to make a short story and it was a great way to meet new people."*

**Áine O'Halloran**, *Breaking Focus* (St. Caimin's Community School, Shannon)
Áine is currently studying Science at the National University of Ireland, Galway. She was a 16 year-old 5th Year student when she participated in the course. Áine has a huge interest in Irish dancing and has been with the Brady-Mullins school of dance for over 16 years. She has kept this

interest going in NUIG, where she is an active member of Dansoc. She also likes calligraphy and will (in her own words) 'read anything you put in front of me'. And, hearteningly (again in her own words), 'I still enjoy writing and have kept it up'.

*"I thought the course was really good. It gave me a chance to experience the work that goes into a short story. It also encouraged me to keep up writing and gave me the skills to edit and critique my own work. It was great to work with Ré, who had so much experience and wisdom to offer."*

**Seán Reddan**, *The Memory* (Meánscoil na mBráithre, CBS Ennistymon)
Seán was 14 and in 2nd Year when he was a participant in the course. He is currently pursuing his Leaving Cert studies at CBS Ennistymon. Seán is an avid soccer player and a big Arsenal supporter. He likes music, particularly electronic and progressive. Crime and war novels are his choices in reading. His favourite author is Stephen King, whom he likes because of his particular ability to write about (in Seán's own words) 'very ordinary people in extraordinary situations'.

*"I thought the course was a great experience. I obtained a lot of valuable information on creative writing skills. I found Ré to be very inspiring. I felt the course sparked an interest in me to write more."*

**Jason Roche**, *Armageddon* (Kilrush Community School)
Currently in 5th Year at Kilrush Community School, Jason was a 13 year-old 2nd Year student when he wrote his story. His hobbies include reading comic books, playing video games and watching television. He is also keenly engaged by punk rock, movies and cars.

*"I found the course very interesting. I enjoyed learning how to develop an idea into a finished story and, in particular, the reading of the finished works."*

**Calem Roelofs**, *Gravity* (Meánscoil na mBráithre, CBS Ennistymon)
Calem was aged 13 and in 2nd Year when he penned *Gravity*. He continues his studies at CBS Ennistymon. Calem shows versatility in his range of hobbies, being interested in skateboarding, reading, making music and, of course, writing.

> *"The course was thoroughly enjoyable. I learned a vast amount about creative writing and it has stood to me in my English studies."*


**Ruádhan Slevin**, *Sniper* (St. Caimin's Community School, Shannon)
Ruádhan was a 15 year-old Junior Cert student when taking the course and he has since gone on to become a mechanic. Ruádhan's major interest is in cars and auto repairs, and he is currently engaged in a major repair project on his own car. He is (and I give his words) 'now an avid reader and, hopefully, would like to write more stories some day'.

> *"I believe this workshop with Ré Ó Laighléis improved my creative writing skills and subsequently helped me in my Junior and Leaving Cert exams. It has inspired me to read more. Also, to this day, I find it easier to express myself in writing."*


**Sabrina Vaughan**, *The Incident* (Ennistymon Vocational School)
Sabrina is still a student in Ennistymon Vocational School and was a 13 year-old 1st Year student when she wrote *The Incident*. Her hobbies include spending time with her family, horse riding, baking with her mother and enjoying life.

> *"I thought the course was very educational and will be a very useful tool to me in my future."*


**Alicia von Metzradt**, *Heartache* (St. Patrick's Comprehensive School, Shannon)
Alicia took the course and wrote her story *Heartache* when she was a 14 year-old 2nd Year student. She has continued on to Leaving Cert in St. Patrick's Comprehensive School. Alicia enjoys reading and listening to music. She has a particular liking for science fiction, poetry, rock and techno music. She also enjoys reading and writing Irish, telling us that

'One day I would like to be fluent *agus, mar a deir an seanfhocal, "Is maith an scéalaí an aimsir".'*

> *"Getting a chance to work with such an esteemed writer as Ré Ó Laighléis was amazing – one of the best things I've done, no doubt. Now, having my story published is simply magical."*

**Emma Waldron**, *Her Story* (Scoil Mhuire, Ennistymon)
Emma's story – the aptly titled *Her Story* – was written when she was a 12 year-old 1st Year student and participant in the course. She loves to read and, of course, write. She takes her inspiration for her writing from her involvement in drama and her strolls in the countryside with her trusted companion, Lucky. Emma also loves performing and is a member of the Clare Youth Theatre, in whose annual productions she is involved.

> *"The course was great. It was fun and it really helped improve my writing skills. Ré really gave us an insight into the world of writers and gave us a taste of life as a professional author."*

# About the Course Director

Ré Ó Laighléis is a native of Sallynoggin, Co. Dublin. A former teacher at primary, secondary and university levels, he left that profession in 1992 to pursue a career in full-time writing. He took his primary degree in Sociology and Gaeilge at Galway University (now NUIG) in 1978. His postgraduate qualifications in Education are from St. Patrick's College of Education, Drumcondra (G.D.Ed., 1980) and Boston College, Massachusetts (M.Ed., 1983). He is a registered Consultant Reading Specialist with the Massachusetts State Board of Education (1983).

Ré writes in the various genres in both English and Irish, and for the child, teenage and adult readerships. He has been the recipient of numerous awards, both nationally and internationally, and his works have been widely translated into many languages. The Arts Council of Ireland has awarded him bursaries in literature on three occasions and he has been Writer-in-Residence in many institutions, including Mayo County Council (1999), the National University of Ireland, Galway (2001) and the Ionad Cultúrtha Arts Centre, Baile Mhúirne (2011). Over the past 20 years, Ré has conducted intensive creative writing courses for adult and teenage writers here in Ireland, in Britain and North America. He is a founder member of MÓINÍN and is currently Director of the company's purpose-built writers' training centre, *An Scríobhlann*, where he gives writing courses in English and Irish to aspiring writers and teachers of those languages.

Though Ré's initial writings were in drama and six of his plays won the All-Ireland Schools Drama title in the 1980s, his concentration since then has been on prose. Amongst his collections are the multi-translated *Ecstasy and other stories*, *Heart of Burren Stone*, *Punk*, *Bolgchaint agus scéalta eile*, *Goimh agus scéalta eile* and many others. He is also the compiler and editor of the teenage-written collection

*Shooting from the Lip*. His novels include *Hooked, Terror on the Burren, Battle for the Burren, Gafa* (which is currently on the Leaving Certificate course), *Osama, Obama, Ó, a Mhama!, The Great Book of the Shapers – A right kick-up in the Arts* and umpteen others. In recent years, in collaboration with the artist AnnMarie McCarthy, he has also concentrated on the very young reader and has written the texts for the bilingual *Fungie* series – *Fungie* (with DVD, 2010/2011), *Fungie & Mara* (2011) and *Fungie & An Tine Mhór* (2012). And a further recent collaboration between the two has seen the publication of *An Coileach a Chailleann a Ghlór* (2012).

Ré, who has lived in Ballyvaughan since 1992, is a regular visitor to schools nationwide under Poetry Ireland's Writers in Schools Scheme, (www.poetryireland.ie) and under the MÓINÍN Visits Scheme (www.moinin.ie).